I0583836

Forgotten Deeds

A Cunning Folk Mystery
Book 2

Prudence S Thomas

Dedication

To the many good friends who have encouraged me to continue writing. Thank you.

Acknowledgments

With many thanks to my editor, Susan Cunningham
and cover designer, Rena at Cover Quill.

Author's Note

The Cunning Folk Mysteries are set in a fantasy version of Lancashire, with a different history to our own. I wanted to be able to explore what life would have been like for men and women who could be described as magical practitioners in an alternate history where Christianity had not spread widely after the fall of the Roman Empire. In my imagined old England (which I have named Albion), there is a strong emphasis on trade and scholarly excellence, rather than on colonialism. Meanwhile the rest of Europe has begun to reach out into the world under the banners of Christian missionaries, placing Albion in a precarious position.

I have taken some liberties with Lancastrian place names for my invented world. Apologies to any Lancastrians or lovers of Lancashire who notice this – consider it a homage to your lovely land's fascinating landscape and history.

Prudence S Thomas

Chapter 1

The embers of a dying fire crackled in the wide stone fireplace of Horn Cottage. Meryall looked around at the cosy interior of the cave house. The warm light touched the smooth whitewashed curve of the rock above her and danced on the jars and pots of herbs on the dresser. She would miss her home over the coming months. Of course, she could drop by every week or so – it was not so far to Poltun, but she had lived in the cottage for all of her life. Spending the chief part of autumn and winter away from its familiar sights and sounds: the shift of the seasons in the woods around the cottage and in her garden, the daily rhythm of her work… Meryall sighed. She had often craved the opportunity to travel, to advance her knowledge, to be, for a short time, free from the responsibility of being the cunning woman for Thornton Cleveleys, but now it was time to take the first small step towards this, she felt reluctant to leave the comfort and familiarity of her home.

She carried the final remaining fresh goods from her stores – the last of her oat bread – into the garden. Meryall stood at her gate and broke the bread into smaller pieces, placing them on the flat top of her gatepost. A crow flew down and settled on the post, pecking away at the bread, one bright black eye focused on Meryall as he ate. She smiled. 'Well, crow, I am going to stay with Arledge until midwinter. Arledge's apprentice, Turi, will look after the house for me. I will ask him to leave food for you if the weather is bitter.' The crow continued to eat. Meryall turned away and went back inside to check that all was as it should be.

Meryall took out her quill and ink and wrote out a detailed list of instructions and advice for Turi: reminders of the various complaints and ailments of the villagers that she had treated recently, requests to ensure he rotated various jars and bottles in the stores as they matured and a myriad of other tasks she was sure he would have the common sense to pursue. The letter, she admitted to herself, was more for her own peace of mind than anything else. The people of Poltun liked Turi and Arledge trusted him. He would do a fine job of taking care of Thornton Cleveleys until she returned. Meryall acknowledged that Turi was more skilful, despite his status as apprentice to Arledge, than she and that the village may in fact be in better hands in her absence. She shrugged off this thought – Thornton was the home of her family and her ancestors had been cunning folk here for many generations. What she lacked in knowledge, she made up for in her deep understanding of the place and people.

Meryall took a couple of bottles of her finest parsnip wine from her stores as a gift for Arledge and rolled them carefully in one of her shifts, placing them upright in the top of the woven willow pack she usually used to carry her herbs and charms to market. She put on a shawl, pinned close to her neck and face beneath her red woollen cloak – the air had a decided bite to it – and pulled on a thick pair of mittens. She settled the pack on her back and stepped out, locking the door behind her and placing the key under a stone near the gate. Turi would be coming over to look after the cottage as well as the village in her absence.

The journey to Poltun was not long – it was only around three miles from Thornton Cleveleys. The route took her inland and through the woods. Meryall was glad to be walking through the woods rather than on the exposed coastline. A fierce wind had blown up soon after she set off, howling around the tops of the trees. It was almost the last day of October and the trees still carried most of their leaves, protecting Meryall from the worst of the wind's power. Despite this, the cold was searching and the bitter chill found each and every gap in her clothing, blowing icy, probing fingers into the neck of her dress and the cuffs of her sleeves. Meryall set down her pack and tucked her sleeves more firmly into her mittens and repinned her shawl under her cloak, pulling it up to wrap it tightly around her face and across her chest to shield her from the cold. Bending to check the lacing of her boots before continuing, Meryall saw a single white speck fall onto the path at her feet. Picking up her pack, she looked up at the sky. It had grown milky white. A flake of snow tumbled down, followed by another and another. A dense flurry of large, feathery flakes filled the air. Meryall frowned. It was early in the season for snow. She estimated that she was just over halfway to Poltun. It would be better to continue on to Arledge's house than to turn back.

Meryall thought of Arledge's house – a rambling stone building with a thatched roof that drooped over a porch of rough-hewn tree trunks. Its immense inglenook fireplace with chairs placed around the hearth would be a welcome sight today. She turned her attention back to the road. The path was already whitening – it was startling how quickly the downfall obscured the world around her. Meryall looked down at her feet as she walked on, eyes narrowed against the wind and cold. The large flakes fell in the forest with an audible patter that was almost like the sizzle of hot fat.

A brown hare broke from the cover of the trees, bounding across Meryall's path in fright. She looked into the forest, curious to see what had startled the hare. Hearing twigs breaking and feet pounding, she spun around, cloak flaring, unable to trace the direction of the noise through the heavy blizzard. Finally, her eyes found movement amongst the trees. A figure stumbled out of the forest, crashing to the ground on the path, breathing heavily, eyes wide. Between the patches of snow sticking to his clothing and hair, Meryall could see smudges of blood on his face and hands. Dark stains covered his clothing. Heart thundering in her chest, she edged towards him, hands outstretched.

Moving closer, Meryall saw that the man was young – he had wide blue eyes, light brown hair, matted and tousled. Under the dirt, his face looked boyish and freckled.

'Easy, friend, I mean you no harm.' She stepped close to him, placing a hand on his arm. 'It appears both you and I are in need of shelter. I know of a woodman's hut near here, come.' She pulled gently at him. He allowed her to lead him, stumbling against her as he faltered on his feet, his eyes fixed on her face.

The snow had become so heavy that Meryall did not think they could continue on safely. It was easy to become lost even in familiar surroundings in weather this poor. She had marked her position well as the snow started to fall and knew the hut was less than a hundred yards off to the right of the path. She guided the man, chatting casually to him, to reassure him, when she could spare breath. Their clothes were beginning to stiffen with the snow and Meryall's face stung with the cold. The man was shivering – Meryall could not tell whether this was from the effects of the temperature alone or whether he was suffering from shock. They bent low as the snow blasted into their faces, making it impossible to see more than a few feet ahead. Meryall reached out to trace the familiar energies of the trees as they went – for she could make out little with her physical vision. She kept up the cheerful patter as they went, although the wind whipped away her words and the effort of their movement hampered her breathing. She had begun to fear she had mistaken the path when she caught sight of the hut. Visibility was so poor that they were almost upon it before she could make out the wooden walls. She felt near to weeping with relief. She pushed the door open and ushered the man inside, closing the door against the driving snow. The communal hut was simple – the hunters of the area used it as a place to eat their meals, warm up in cold weather and share stories and a drink after a successful hunt. A table and chairs hewn from forest timber, well worn by use, furnished the hut. Meryall looked at her companion. He was shivering and looking around the hut in bewilderment. She gently removed his cloak and steered him to a chair she placed in front of the fireplace. Searching through the store cupboard, Meryall found old, frayed blankets. The hut also functioned as a place for the hunters' communal celebrations at the start or end of the season, when such enthusiastic feasting and drinking happened that they often chose to sleep in the hut rather than brave what became a long walk when drunk. She wrapped a blanket around the man's shoulders, placing another on his lap. It relieved Meryall to see that the log store was well stocked and that a basket of kindling stood on the hearth. She took her flint from her pack and laid a fire. The dry, seasoned firewood caught easily and soon sent forth waves of warmth that made Meryall's cold fingers ache. She could not remember being more grateful for a fire.

The light danced on the homely interior of the hut. The closely shuttered windows held firm against the storm, but Meryall could still hear the wind whirling snow against the sturdy wooden walls.

She turned her attention to the stranger seated before her. He was gazing at the fire, but trembling violently, his blankets clutched to his chest.

Meryall returned to the store cupboard and stood on the tips of her toes, probing the back of the top shelf. She smiled. As she had expected – emergency rations. She pulled out a dusty, squat bottle. She removed the stopper and sniffed. The potent scent of moorland whisky filled her nose. Taking down two rough cups, Meryall poured generous measures. She put a cup into the man's hands. He looked at her for a moment before lifting the cup between his shaking hands and taking a jerking gulp of whisky. The fiery spirit made him cough, but Meryall could see a hint of colour return to his cheeks.

'My name is Meryall,' she said, keeping her voice soft and unhurried.

The man looked at her for a long moment,

appearing puzzled. 'My name…' he began, his voice cracked and rasping. He coughed and tried to clear his throat, taking another drink. 'My name is…' He looked at Meryall, seemingly confused and beginning to become distressed. 'What is my name?'

'I don't know, but I am sure it will come back to you,' Meryall said, hiding her concern in a show of cheerfulness. 'Now, let me look at your wounds and we will see if we can make you more comfortable.'

Meryall searched through her pack and brought out a package of herbs and a cloth. A kettle hung from a hook on the wall. She carried it to the doorway and opened the door a crack. The wind blew snow hard into her face. Meryall crouched and scooped snow into the kettle, using the snow to scour it briefly before emptying and refilling it. Her face stinging with cold, she shut the door firmly against the storm and hung the kettle over the fire, busying herself to distract from the thoughts that crowded in upon her. Who was this young man? And how came he to be wandering in such a condition through the cold? What could possibly have befallen him?

Chapter 2

Meryall stood and watched the snow in the kettle melt. The intense cold had created snowflakes like tiny stars – the individual shape of each flake visible against her cloak until they winked away into drops of moisture in the warmth of the fire. Meryall took dried marigold from her pack and placed the golden petals into a pot. She checked the kettle. The snow had finally melted, but the icy water took time to boil. She bustled around the little hut gathering her tools.

'The snow came in very suddenly today, did it not?' she said cheerfully.

The man nodded.

'I had not far to go, but I think we did well to seek shelter.'

The man looked attentively at Meryall, but said nothing.

'I have known this hut since I was a girl. You should see the celebrations the Thornton Cleveleys hunters have had over the years!' Meryall chuckled. 'There have been times where scarcely a hunter in the village has been able to rise and stand upright in the morning, after the drinking and feasting they have seen.'

'Thornton Cleveleys?' The man's voice was stronger than before, but Meryall noticed that his tone and accent were gentle and refined.

'Yes, that is my village. We are not far from there. Do you recognise the name?' Meryall studied his face.

'I— no. I don't think so, it seemed like I should know the place for a moment, but now I cannot recollect why I should know the name at all.'

Meryall took the steaming kettle from the stove and poured the water over the petals. The steam rose to kiss her face with warmth and the familiar, strong, woody, floral scent of marigold. She covered the pot to keep in the healing properties of the flowers as the mixture cooled.

Meryall took up their cups and placed a few dried lemon verbena leaves in each, a spoonful of honey, from the jar taken from deep in her pack – a keepsake to remind her of her hives – and a generous glug of whisky, before adding the remaining hot water from the kettle to top up the cups. She stirred them with a quick hand and took a seat next to her unexpected charge, putting his cup into his hands with the brisk instruction to drink. He took a sip from the cup and smiled at Meryall, his face showing boyish dimples.

'Thank you, mistress,' he said, breathing the scent

from his cup deeply, pressing his fingers against the warm, coarse pottery.

Although his nails were dirty, his hands were slim, with long, elegant fingers.

Meryall regarded him closely. His clothes, though torn and dirty, appeared to be of fair quality – plain and unembellished, but well-made and of good cloth. It was difficult to judge his age under the dirt and blood, but she took him to be young – no more than twenty or so years old. He was not handsome, but his face was pleasing and fresh, despite the grazes and mud. She sensed goodness in him and wondered what had happened to this young man.

'Tell me, what can you remember about how you came to be here?' she said lightly. The man put down his cup and looked down at his hands, rubbing at the dirt and blood, without appearing to see them.

'I remember an inn. A pleasant place – a handsome young woman with dark hair serving me a good meal before a blazing fire … there was a sign – a sun.'

Meryall leaned forward eagerly. 'A sun, did you say?'

The man nodded. Meryall sat back. The Sunn Inn in Samlesbury – she knew it well. It was miles from here, however, too far away for the stranger to have walked in his current condition.

She pattered on, telling the stranger about her plans for the winter, the village and remarking on the unusual weather. He seemed soothed by her voice, or perhaps by the sense of normality her inconsequential chat gave him.

Meryall rose and picked up the pot of herbs, checking the temperature. It had infused for long enough and the water was cool enough for her to dip a clean cloth into to start cleaning the stranger's wounds. Meryall checked him over. There was blood on his face and on the back of his head. The blood on his face seemed to consist of smears from where he had touched his head and bloodied his hands, transferring the blood to wherever he touched. She gently started to clean away the dried blood from his hair so she could see the injury underneath. The stranger sat quietly as she worked, his eyes lowered meekly to the ground. Parting the thick brown hair, Meryall saw a jagged cut and a swelling. She frowned. He may have fallen and hit his head, but the wound was high on his crown. If he had fallen, the wound would have been likely to be more to the back of his head. Perhaps he had tripped and hit his head against a low branch? Meryall looked closely at the bloody line. The flesh was pink and healthy-looking – there was no infection, although the skin around the swollen bump had blackened with bruising under his hair. Meryall cleaned the blood from his neck – it had trickled down his head and onto the back of his tunic. Meryall stood back, looking at the man before her, checking him for injuries. Although there was a good deal of blood on the front of his tunic, she could not trace where it had come from. There was too much of it to have come from him touching his head and wiping his hands on his chest and she could not see any signs that the blood had come from a cut or wound to the man's torso. She frowned, deep in thought.

A crunching sound outside the hut startled her. The stranger started up from his chair. They stood in silence for a long moment. The rhythmic crunch, crunch came again.

'Meryall!' The shout came from a strong male voice, right by the door of the hut.

'Yes!' Meryall replied, rushing to pull the door open, snow cascading onto the floor as she looked out into the blinding whiteness.

A group of people stood in the snow, swathed in cloaks and thick clothing. Arledge stepped forward and enfolded her in a hug. After him came a woman and two men-at-arms, who entered talking excitedly.

'We hoped you had made it as far as the hut, but feared the storm had stranded you on the road—' Arledge began, his voice halting as he noticed the stranger seated by the fire, eyeing him cautiously.

There was a heavy silence as the party looked at the stranger's bloodied clothes.

'I am not the only one caught out by the storm, you see!' said Meryall, her voice sounding bright and brittle in the still room. 'I was just finishing cleaning this man's head wound – he was wandering in confusion after a blow to the head – it is lucky that our paths crossed, or he may have perished in the snow, in his state of bewilderment.' Meryall looked at the faces around her with concern – their hands were on the hilts of their swords and their eyes were hard.

'I do not believe I have met your friends,' Meryall said, turning to Arledge.

Arledge gestured to the tall, red-headed woman at his side. 'This is Dye Brereton, sheriff of Poltun and her men, Barnard and Hew.'

'I am pleased to meet you,' Meryall said, taking each of their hands in turn.

'Your wounds must be grave, sir,' Dye said, her eyes fixed on the stranger's bloodied tunic. 'I cannot recall your face. Where are you from?'

The man looked up in panic and confusion, beginning to stutter out a reply. Meryall went to his side and placed a hand on his shoulder.

'I believe the blow somewhat scrambled his wits,' she said, motioning Dye over to examine the wound. 'He cannot recall his name or the place he calls home.'

'Indeed, that is a nasty injury,' Dye replied. She stepped back and took a long look at the man. 'Are you hurt elsewhere? There is a great deal of blood on you.'

'I-I do not believe so, Sheriff,' the stranger said, looking down at himself as if seeing the stains on his clothes for the first time and running his hands over his stomach and sides.

Arledge beckoned Meryall to him. 'Are you certain he is what he seems? It may be that he feigns forgetfulness to deflect from deeds he himself would rather forget. How did he come to be covered in such a quantity of blood?'

Meryall looked over his shoulder at the stranger. Despite the circumstances, she could not sense any evil in him, only confusion and fear.

'We have no evidence of any wrongdoing. I cannot think of any action we can take other than to care for him hoping he recovers and can recall how he came to be wandering alone in the forest. He said the last thing he remembers was being at the Sunn Inn in Samlesbury, but the roads are too poor for us to send word to Eda to find out what she knows of this man,' she said.

Arledge shrugged. 'Have a care, Meryall, you are too quick to trust,' he said.

'Do you sense any malevolence in him?' she asked.

Arledge was silent for a long moment, regarding the stranger thoughtfully. 'No, I cannot say I do, yet even the best of men may commit a terrible act.'

'Well, we must treat him as an innocent man until there is reason to believe him to be otherwise.' Meryall set her mouth in a firm line.

Arledge smiled. 'You remind me of your mother,' he said, touching her arm softly. 'I see you had got out cups – is there anything good left for us to drink? We had a cold journey in search of you. We may as well warm ourselves before we return to Poltun. The snow has stopped falling, but it is bitterly cold and the drifts lie deep.'

Meryall sighed. She had to admit she understood Arledge and Dye's caution.

'Yes, the hunters always keep the hut well stocked. We must return when the weather improves to refill their whisky bottle.' She took more cups from the shelf and poured generous measures.

'He will need to stay somewhere whilst he recovers,' she said, handing Arledge his cup.

Arledge arched an eyebrow. 'And I suppose that you would suggest that he stays at my house?'

Meryall nodded. 'You are a talented healer. Where else could he be cared for so well?'

Arledge frowned a little. 'The sheriff has secure chambers where we could visit him to treat him.'

'Chambers?' Meryall snorted. 'That is a grand name for a cell. You would send a sick man, who we have no evidence has committed any unlawful act, to a dungeon?'

'You are being overdramatic. He will be cared for and observed within the sheriff's keep.'

'You are capable of performing a binding spell to ensure that he does not harm anyone, are you not?' Meryall persisted.

Arledge narrowed his eyes. 'You ask a lot of me, Meryall.'

'I ask that you act as the just man I know you to be,' she said.

Arledge looked around the room. Dye, her men and the stranger were all watching them. The stranger's eyes were huge and round, rimmed with the red of exhaustion.

Arledge inclined his head. 'Very well. For now, he will stay at my house, if you are happy with that, Dye?'

Dye nodded. 'I do not doubt that you can keep him from causing harm, should he wish to do so, until we have a clearer idea of how he came to be situated thus.'

An uneasy quiet filled the hut whilst they finished their drinks and made preparations to depart. Barnard and Hew carried a pack with extra clothing, brought in case Meryall had been ill-equipped for the cold. She refused an extra cloak, holding up her woollen cloak to show how thick it was, giving it instead to the stranger, who wore only a long tunic over linen breeches.

Meryall saw the men exchange glances as she handed the garment to the stranger. 'We will of course wash it before we return it to the sheriff's keep, if you are worried about getting blood on it,' she said coolly.

Dye opened the door. The cold washed over them immediately. A light wind was blowing, picking up the snow and swirling it into clouds above the ground. Their tracks were still visible.

'Stay close together and watch your footing,' Dye instructed.

They pulled the door firmly shut and walked carefully back onto the road, following their tracks back on the path to Poltun. Barnard and Hew shadowed the stranger closely, their burly figures imposing in contrast to his slender frame. Meryall could see him looking at them anxiously out of the sides of his eyes, his gaze drawn to the swords at their waists. Meryall moved forward to walk next to the stranger. She smiled to reassure him. 'You will find a good fire and a warm bed at Arledge's house,' she said. 'We shall all be glad of a good night's sleep, I daresay.'

The stranger gave a faltering smile in return, nodding gratefully. He was shivering once again. Anger brought warm blood to her cheeks as she looked at the sheriff and guards. Wyot, her own sheriff, would not have been so hard on so vulnerable a wanderer had the stranger chanced to have been found in Thornton Cleveleys.

Chapter 3

The deep snow made every step on the road to Poltun arduous and their boots and clothing quickly became heavy with snow, with some finding its way through every gap at the tops of their boots to chill their legs, feet and ankles more and more thoroughly. The wind threw up eddies of snow from time to time, stinging their eyes and faces. Meryall pulled her shawl tightly around her hair and up over her nose and mouth, but the cold still filled her ears and chilled her very soul.

She could not recall a mile and a half feeling so long. Dye and her men accompanied them to Arledge's threshold, then continued on to the sheriff's keep, in search of good fires, roasted meat and ale.

Meryall looked up at the house. Arledge's home was an old thatched house with a gnarled wood porch. The ancient wings of the house rambled away in a ramshackle mass of gables, added by generation upon generation of Poltun cunning folk. As she had remembered, a lantern hung at the apex above the front door, casting a dim light out into the pure white of the garden.

She felt tears pricking at her eyes. Puzzled, she looked within herself, seeking the origin of the rush of emotion. It was impossible to step inside Arledge's home without remembering her mother and that it was the loss of her mother that had left her in need of Arledge's tuition.

Arledge shoved the door open, shouting out to his housekeeper to bring hot ale and to take their sodden cloaks from them. Meryall sniffed. The smell of baking apples and spice permeated the air. Arledge's housekeeper Alys, a slim, wiry woman in her middle years, came forward and removed their cloaks, taking them to dry before the kitchen fire. Arledge, Meryall and the stranger sank into the high-backed chairs in the shelter of the large inglenook fireplace. Meryall's muscles pulsed with fatigue. The cold seeped out of her as the fire warmed her flesh. The warmth, almost overwhelming, filled her with intense pleasure. Alys returned with a tray of foaming mugs of lambswool: spiced, sweetened ale topped with the white baked apple flesh that gave the drink its name. It was one of Meryall's favourites. It smelled like autumn and she reflected that she usually associated the scent with crisp, sunny days. Snow so early in the season could mean a long, hard winter. The villagers would not be able to forage for fruit as they normally would and neither would the birds and animals.

Meryall breathed in the scent of the lambswool, allowing herself to become lost in the pleasure of the taste and aroma for a few moments. She sighed, tired after the unexpected stress of the day. Arledge would be keen to perform a binding spell before they retired for the evening and she knew it was important that she observed his work, regardless of how she felt about it. She followed him to his study.

'How can you bind the stranger, Arledge? I thought it was essential to know a man's name in order to bind him,' Meryall said, watching him gather items from the many shelves, drawers and boxes around the room.

'There are other ways,' Arledge replied. 'Observe.'

He took out a small piece of vellum and drew a figure in the centre. Although the details were sparse, Meryall recognised the figure as that of the stranger, from the mop of hair and tattered clothes. Around the stranger's form, Arledge drew a circle. He sprinkled a black powder onto the circle and folded the vellum with the powder within it.

Arledge pulled his knife from his belt and measured out three lengths of black thread. He tied a piece of thread around the little package, whispering words into his hands as he knotted the thread once, twice, three times. He repeated the charm again and again with the two remaining pieces of thread, until the square of vellum was bound all around with dark, knotted lines.

Arledge stood and took a long steel pin from his

desk. With the pin, he pierced the square and fastened it to the mantlepiece above his fire.

Meryall stared at it. 'My mother told me that it was wrong to attempt to bind another person's power unless it was absolutely clear that it was for the greater good and there was no alternative.'

'Your mother was a fine woman, as are you,' Arledge replied, his blue eyes cold. 'But she understood, as I am sure you eventually will, that there are times when one must protect others. Our stranger will come to no harm if he means no harm. I have merely bound him from hurting others and have secured him to this house until I bid him to leave.'

Meryall swallowed the reply that rose in her throat. She was certain that she was not mistaken and that her mother would not have approved of his actions.

It was unfortunate, she reflected, that her apprenticeship seemed destined to begin with acrimony and disagreement.

The morning was cold and crisp. No more snow had fallen overnight, but a thick layer still covered the ground and the pale sun shimmered on icicles along the edges of the roof. Meryall stood in the porch looking out. She loved the quiet that snow brought to the world. It was a reminder of the goddess. Man was powerless against the might of nature. Her thoughts turned to Madoc. She had missed his warmth and the comfort of his calm presence last night, alone in a chamber high in Arledge's attics. He would have opened the shop by now. The cold weather would send many villagers to him for remedies for chilblains and aching bones. What would he make of this stranger? She would value his opinion both on the man's wound and on his character. She did not know the Poltun apothecary well, although Madoc met with him from time to time to trade herbs, equipment and talk of favoured recipes.

She found Arledge and the stranger sitting in the kitchen when she went back indoors.

'A fine day,' Meryall said, smiling at them both cheerfully. The stranger was quiet, hunched over a steaming bowl of porridge. Meryall sat next to him, adding stewed plums to her own bowl of porridge and pouring a cup of tisane from the pot. She sniffed. The tisane contained ginger and juniper berry. Meryall grinned into her cup. For all Arledge's show of suspicion towards the stranger, the herbs he had chosen, whilst warming and appropriate for the weather, also combatted memory loss and helped fight dizziness and fatigue, such as those who had suffered a head injury might experience.

'I will walk into the village and ask the apothecary, Fujikawa, to come out to us, to check you over,' she said to the stranger as they finished their meal.

He smiled. 'Thank you. I am sorry to cause you trouble. I would walk with you to save the apothecary the journey, but I am feeling dizzy and my head aches.'

'It is no problem. I will enjoy a visit to Fujikawa's shop and he and Arledge are old friends, so he will not mind coming over.'

Meryall collected her outer garments from the drying rack next to the fire. She relished the warmth against her skin as she wrapped herself in her shawl and cloak and put on her mittens. She borrowed a stick from the stand by the door and set out. It was only half a mile to the village and she was glad of the fresh air.

The early snow hung heavy on trees still jewelled with autumn fruit and the fields lay smoothed under an eiderdown of white.

Poltun was a pretty, lively village with a cluster of buildings around the central marketplace. It had a large thatched inn, popular with merchants and sailors and was often rowdy after they had spent their newly earned coin on much ale. Despite the weather, the villagers were busy clearing a space and gathering wood for the great bonfire for the Samhain celebrations the following day.

Fujikawa's apothecary shop occupied a sizeable corner building with windows on two sides displaying his wares. Meryall opened the door, setting a brass bell jingling.

Fujikawa sat at a desk near the fire, measuring out herbs. He looked up at her entrance and stood to welcome her.

'Mistress Meryall? It has been many years since I last

saw you. Arledge told me we were to have the pleasure of your presence in Poltun for the winter. Can I offer you a drink and a seat before the fire?'

Meryall thanked him gratefully. She was chilled to the bone, despite her warm layers of clothing. Fujikawa pulled a chair close to the fire and poured small measures of a dark golden liquid into two cups, placing them on the hearth to warm.

'How is Madoc?' he enquired.

'Well – he hopes to pay you a visit soon,' Meryall replied.

Fujikawa nodded. 'I will be glad to see him, we always have many remedies and stories to share when we meet, which is too seldom, in my opinion.'

'I have come to ask a favour,' Meryall said, picking up her cup. 'I came upon a stranger on the road yesterday, lost in the heavy snow. He had met with a misfortune of some kind and was walking in a state of confusion after a blow to the head. He cannot recall his name nor where he came from, at present.'

Fujikawa frowned. 'Indeed! How severe is the wound in his head?'

Meryall shrugged. 'I have examined it as best I can. There is a swelling and a jagged cut, but I do not think his skull is broken and there are no signs of an infection at present. Arledge gave him ginger and juniper tea this morning and I have cleaned the wound with calendula, but otherwise, we have left nature to heal him thus far.'

'Has he been sick or lost consciousness?'

'Not in the time we have seen him. He is dizzy and had pain in his head this morning. He had clotted blood on his head when I met with him, so the injury may have happened some time before I found him.'

'I see,' Fujikawa said. 'Well, we shall take our drinks and allow you to warm up before we set out for Arledge's house. What type of person do you take this stranger to be?'

Meryall sipped her drink appreciatively. It was a rich, good-quality mead, well-aged. She savoured the spreading warmth it brought to her throat and chest for a moment whilst she thought.

'There are no callouses on his hands and his garments are well cut and of good cloth. His manner is gentle and his accent refined. I do not believe him to be a farmer or fisherman. The last place he remembers being is the Sunn Inn at Samlesbury. We must wait for the weather to improve before we can make enquiries there, or for his wits to return, to know more, whichever is soonest.'

Draining his drink, Fujikawa stood and pulled a battered leather bag from under the desk. He took portions of roots and herbs from the jars on his shelves, decanting them into smaller pots.

'Madoc tells me you grow several herbs he has only previously been able to purchase from merchants coming from the East,' Meryall said, watching him with interest. 'I hope that the cold will not damage your plants.'

Fujikawa shook his head. 'Thankfully, a number of the plants I have gathered on my travels relish the cold and the shade of the woods here; indeed some come from the high mountains of my own country and will revel in the reminder of their home that this weather will bring. They will be fine. I will visit them when the snow thaws to check, but I expect that they will be well able to survive these conditions.'

Fujikawa finished filling his bag and went into the back of the shop to put on warm clothing. He returned with a fur hat, sturdy boots and a thick wool cloak. They stepped out onto the street. Fujikawa turned the sign on the door to 'out' and locked it behind them.

They picked their way between the patches of compacted snow that had started to make the well-trodden paths of the town treacherous. The fresher snow on the lane to Arledge's house came as a relief.

'Madoc tells me you lived in Russia and travelled widely before you came to Poltun. What was it like? I have a great desire to travel,' Meryall said, able to chat now it was easier to walk.

Fujikawa smiled. 'I left Hiroshima – the Broad Island, you would call it in English – with a Portuguese doctor. We parted company, amicably, in Lisbon and I wandered on through Spain, France, Germany, Norway and eventually reached Russia. I had no real purpose in my journeying. I spent time with physicians and healers, gathering seeds and writing down the remedies they shared with me, but not all of the world is as fond of foreigners as I have found your land to be.'

Meryall frowned. 'You found nowhere you could settle happily?'

Fujikawa shook his head. 'No, in Russia, I made a fine living as a physician to the nobility, but I had to leave after one of my patients died – poisoned in a plot nothing at all to do with me – after which I stood accused of witchcraft and fled with only my medicines and the small items of value I could carry with me, which was little enough.'

'And what brought you to Albion and to Poltun?'

'I had met Arledge in the markets of Lisbon and became friends with him. He told me of the tolerant nature of your people and I retained the impression of his goodness and wisdom. It came to the forefront of my mind as I ran from such intolerance and corruption and so I made my way here, eventually earning enough as I crossed through Europe from selling my cures to pay my passage and even amass sufficient money to establish my shop.'

'Arledge must have been both surprised and delighted to see you.'

Fujikawa laughed heartily. 'I have rarely had such a warm welcome. We drank and ate for hours on my first night in Poltun.' He looked sideways at Meryall. 'I expect that Arledge has been friend and guide to many who have needed it over the years.'

Meryall nodded. 'Yes, he was a great support to me after the death of my mother. Indeed, he was a great support to my mother before me. We are fortunate to have someone of such wisdom in our area.'

They passed the rest of the journey discussing the foods, sights and smells that Fujikawa had experienced on his many travels. Fujikawa spoke with animation of the seething, lively ports of Lisbon, where people from almost every part of the world met to trade goods – and every imaginable vice flourished. He spoke of the scent of the spices as trunk after trunk of cinnamon, pepper and nutmeg was unloaded and of the brightness of the silks against the blazing blue skies of the city. He talked with feeling of the human cost of these riches. Though Lisbon was the central point of European trade and had grown rich through the thirst for luxurious goods amongst the European elite, this abundance was also enabled through the trade of people. Slave ships docked there and Fujikawa's descriptions of the suffering of the men, women and children bought, sold and worked to their deaths there brought tears to Meryall's eyes. He spoke with longing of his home town, of the serene mountains and of the art and poetry that flourished in his country. His recollections were tinged with sadness and with anecdotes of human cruelty, but Meryall felt more than ever the irresistible pull of the unknown horizons beyond her village and beyond Albion as she recognised the limits of her own knowledge and experience. The world held much of which she was ignorant, both good and bad.

Arledge was sitting in the kitchen with the stranger when they arrived. The latter was wrapped in a blanket by the fire. He looked pale, but his face brightened when he saw Meryall.

Fujikawa and Arledge embraced briefly, before Fujikawa turned, smiling, to his patient. Arledge went into his study to prepare charms for the villagers who had made requests of him that morning and to ready his supplies for the next day's Samhain celebrations, evidently grateful to reclaim his time.

'Now, friend, tell me, how are you?' Fujikawa pressed and probed and looked into the man's eyes.

'I am … better, thank you,' the stranger said, his voice low and weak.

Fujikawa sat down next to him and asked him many questions. The stranger appeared to want to answer, but Meryall could tell that he was quickly becoming fatigued and he merely shrugged. Fujikawa stood, moving the kettle onto a hook over the fire to bring it to the boil. He moved efficiently around Arledge's kitchen, taking up a cup from the dresser and the pestle and mortar from a cupboard. He withdrew several little jars from his bag and arranged them on the table. He extracted a dried root from one and, pulling his knife from his belt pouch, chopped it into small pieces. He placed it in the mortar and began to pound it into a powder. The smell that rose from it was delicious, floral yet heavy, like incense. Meryall breathed deeply, trying to place it. Fujikawa glanced at her as he worked.

'This root is the pride of Siberia. It is believed to make the people who drink it daily live long lives. I am using it, however, for its usefulness in easing headaches and combating nervous fatigue. It is an unassuming little plant. You will see it flowering all over the rocks in my garden in the summer.'

'Is it native to Albion?' Meryall asked, looking closely at the remaining root in the jar.

'It grows in mountainous places here. However, I brought my seeds with me from Russia.'

Fujikawa took up more jars, adding some dried leaves with a soft, sweet scent to the mortar. Mixing the dried leaves and powdered root, Fujikawa scooped a spoonful into the cup, added a little honey and poured hot water over the herbs, stirring vigorously. He left the cup, covered with a plate, to brew whilst he packed away his jars. He poured the remaining herbs into one of his little containers, scribbling a note on dosage and administration. This done, he put the cup into the stranger's hands.

'Drink, my friend, this will do you good. It will ease your headache and stimulate your memory.' He turned to Meryall. 'He will need much rest and as little stress as possible. I suggest that he is not pressed about what happened. He will regain his memory soon enough.'

Meryall nodded. 'Thank you, Fujikawa. Can I get you some refreshments before you go?'

'You are very kind, however, I will spend time with Arledge in his study before I set off. I daresay he has a bottle of something pleasant tucked away in there somewhere.' He gave a small bow and a wink.

Meryall laughed. She watched him make his way to Arledge's study. She had not previously understood that the men were on such an easy footing. Meryall was pleased that Arledge, who needed warmth and lightness in his life, had a companion.

She turned back to the stranger, who was watching all that passed with a gentle curiosity.

'Well, you heard the advice of our learned friend. I would suggest that you take a nap, I could see you flagging as you talked with Fujikawa. When you awake, I will bring you a cup of broth, if you like.'

'Thank you, that would be pleasant.' The stranger tucked his blanket around him, curling up into his chair like a child. Meryall stoked the fire and went out to the porch to gather apples for the evening's game of apple bobbing. Her breath formed clouds of steam as she worked, picking through the stored fruit and putting the rosiest fruit into her basket. The autumn scent of apples filled her nose, at odds with the unseasonable chill of the air.

The sound of boots crunching through the snow broke her concentration. Meryall leaned on the low wooden gate of the porch and looked out into the lane. Dye and her men were approaching the house. Meryall waved cheerily. Dye gave a salute in return, but did not smile. A throb of apprehension coursed through Meryall. Whatever their business, it was not social.

She opened the gate and stepped out to meet them. 'Greetings, may I offer you a drink? I can warm ale if you would like,' Meryall said politely, eyeing Dye's face closely. Dye did not meet her gaze.

'I thank you, but no. We come on business. Is the stranger still with you?'

Meryall's stomach turned over. She hesitated for a moment. 'Yes, Fujikawa has been treating him. He has yet to regain his memory and is still weak from the blow to his head. I take it this visit is not merely to check on his recovery?'

Dye shook her head. 'A corpse has been found in the woods. The man did not die naturally. There are signs of a violent struggle, with knife wounds to his chest. We have come to take the stranger into custody to question him about the death.'

Meryall breathed in sharply. This was grave news and looked very bad for their guest. Her gut told her that the open, mild young man had played no part in this death, yet how could the blood on his clothing, so clearly not his own, be innocently accounted for in these circumstances?

'Fujikawa has recommended rest. I think it unlikely that the stranger will run. Surely it is unnecessary to take him into custody? There can be no harm in waiting until he recovers, at least.'

Dye shifted her weight uneasily. 'You are kind and honest, Meryall, therefore I believe you see more of these qualities in others than they may deserve. This man is a stranger to us and has arrived in suspicious circumstances. Now we have reason to believe that he may have killed a man and we must assume that he may be a danger to others, until it can be proven otherwise.'

There was the sound of movement behind her. Meryall glanced round. Arledge had emerged from his study, Fujikawa at his heels.

'Come in, Dye,' he said, making space for her to enter with her men. 'You will find the stranger in the kitchen.'

Meryall glared at him. 'You are surely not condoning the stranger being placed in the sheriff's dungeons, Arledge? He is unwell. There is no need to remove him, he has shown no violence or ill intent.'

Arledge shrugged. 'I'm sorry, Meryall. I am unwilling for him to continue in my home under these circumstances. The sheriff has every right to remove him. I will not object.'

Meryall looked desperately at Fujikawa.

'It is unfortunate,' he said, looking at Meryall with sympathy, 'but I will visit him at the sheriff's keep and continue his treatment. Do not worry, Meryall, if he is innocent, all will become apparent.'

Meryall shook her head, anger and disappointment forcing tears to her eyes and bringing a lump to her throat so painful that she could not speak. She pushed past Arledge and went into the kitchen. Dye and her men stood around the stranger. He was sitting looking up at them in surprise, still wrapped in his blankets.

'Put on your boots,' Dye said. 'You are in my custody and will remain at the keep whilst we investigate you for the crime of murder.'

The stranger started as if the sheriff's words caused him physical pain, recoiling in shock. 'Murder? I do not understand!' he said, his voice shaking.

'Come, put on your boots.' Dye said coolly. 'It is not far to the keep.'

He rose meekly and started to pull on his boots, his hands shaking so badly he could not tie the laces. Meryall moved towards him and crouched to help him. 'Do not worry. I will come and see you and Fujikawa will bring you medicine. You may take your blankets with you, as you have no warm clothing of your own.'

The stranger stuttered his thanks, looking dazed and frightened.

'May he at least take a cup of broth before he leaves?' Meryall asked Dye.

'There is no need. I will arrange a meal for him when we arrive at the keep.' Dye's voice was smooth, yet she still did not look Meryall in the eye.

'Come, man, it is time to go.'

Meryall moved in front of Dye's men and arranged the stranger's blankets around his shoulders so he could move easily. 'Take heart. We will come and see you soon,' she said, trying to smile reassurance.

Dye's men took the stranger's elbows and guided him out of the house. The stranger turned his head to look back at Meryall, his eyes huge in his pale face.

'Help me, please,' he whispered.

Meryall's eyes swam with tears. She turned away hurriedly, unwilling to let the others see her distress. She heard the door shut and sank down into the chair by the fire.

Arledge and Fujikawa came into the kitchen. She was aware of their presence, but unable to trust herself to speak to either of them.

Quietly, they returned to the study, leaving Meryall alone before the dying fire.

Chapter 4

S amhain morning arrived. The snow had been trodden into sludge along the well-used paths and roads leading to the village, but still lay thickly on the roof and upon the grass and trees around Arledge's house.

Meryall stood looking out along the road. She had risen early, unable to sleep as she imagined the stranger lying cold and frightened in the sheriff's cells. Her anger at Arledge bubbled under the surface. Her reasonable nature told her that is was unfair to feel angry with him. Arledge's decision was logical, the case for detaining the stranger was hard to refute; however Meryall had sensed the essence of the man and had not detected any malice in him. Her heart rebelled against logic.

She breathed a deep sigh of frustration, her breath forming clouds in the still, cold air. The stranger's arrival had taken her attention away from the reason for her presence here. Today would be a busy day; not only would Arledge require her help in the Samhain celebrations, but it was also time to start their training in earnest. She must trust Dye to investigate properly and Fujikawa to continue with his care for the man. There was nothing more she could do.

She saw a figure, swathed in warm clothing, on the road from the village. Meryall waved and Alys raised her hand in reply.

She turned back into the house and busied herself in stoking the fire and putting the kettle to boil. Arledge would be down soon, hearing Alys arriving.

Alys came into the kitchen, her dour face lit with a smile. Samhain was a great celebration in the village and Alys was proud of her role as Arledge's helper. She was carrying a large basket and began taking out the well-wrapped packages and placing them on the table. There was a loaf of oat bannock bread, still slightly warm, a stoppered pitcher of milk and a dish of poached eggs and boiled onions, covered in melted cheese. Alys tested the temperature of this. Nodding with satisfaction, she placed it on the warming plate of the range to keep warm until Arledge came down.

Arledge swept into the kitchen. He gave Alys a swift kiss on the cheek and a smile, exclaiming over the savoury scent of the dish as it warmed. He nodded coolly to Meryall and bid her good morning. Meryall was glad of Alys's bustle and chatter as she put out dishes for them and fussed over Arledge.

'This morning, Meryall, we start your apprenticeship. I plan to teach you the skill of healing and for that, you need to journey within yourself to understand where you draw strength from to heal others.'

Meryall murmured a respectful acknowledgement. There was little point in aggravating Arledge with discussion about the stranger when she was unsure if her point could even be coherently argued. Arledge would understand the importance of a gut feeling, but he would not agree that she should abide by it in the face of the evidence. What had he told her? Good men may do evil things. She sighed. Perhaps she was wrong after all.

Alys cleared away the plates – Meryall had eaten, but could scarcely recall the flavour of the food. She stood to help Alys, guilty that she had not enjoyed her beautifully cooked meal as she should have.

Arledge beckoned her through to his study. It was a large room with low beams and a thick tree trunk, smooth with age and use, as the mantlepiece across the fireplace. The lively fire threw shadows on piles of parchment, books and obscure objects Arledge had collected on his travels. Meryall moved to his desk. On a stack of writings sat a tiny rounded pottery object, like a flattened jug, with a small round handle, a hole in the top and a hole at the top of the lip shape at the front. It was decorated with a pattern of dots and a slip glaze. Meryall looked at the little thing with a potter's eye. Arledge came to her elbow, smiling as she examined the pot.

'What do you make of it?' he asked.

'Is it an oil lamp?' Meryall asked, tilting her head and frowning.

'Yes, a Roman one – hundreds of years old. Yet if you hold it close to your nose, you can still pick up the scent of the oil that once filled it.'

Meryall held it close to her face, imagining this little lamp lighting the way for a Roman man or woman, so long ago. She sniffed. The smell of the oil was still there, as Arledge had said, a trace of the far-off Roman sunshine which had nourished the olive trees.

'Well, we have work to do,' Arledge said, showing Meryall to a seat by the fire. 'Now, in your previous journeys, you have sought answers for divination, or dream walking, yes?'

Meryall assented.

'This time, you must go within and find the place from which you will draw the energy to heal others – you must find your connection with the earth, with the goddess. You will be shown what you need to understand to take this next step along your path. I will be here when you return, fear not.'

Meryall settled herself into the well-stuffed, worn chair and closed her eyes. She heard Arledge moving around and caught the scent of wormwood smoke from the fire. Breathing the harsh herbal smell deeply, she turned her mind within. Waiting, she focused on Arledge's instructions. She grew taller, wider than her physical body, beginning to drift into the other plane.

The veil between the worlds was thin – Samhain brought the planes close to one another; she could feel the connections between them as fine and delicate as cobwebs. She frowned. A thought snagged against her as she rose, pulling her back into herself. The image of the stranger's face, filled with fear, flashed across her mind, bringing her fully and heavily back to her body. She let out a long breath, seeking to release the sadness and worry that clouded her thoughts and started again and again. Each time, images of the stranger interrupted her journey before it began. She sensed Arledge seated near her. Irritation seeped into her as she became frustrated at each failure. He would know how she was feeling and be able to see her struggle. Abruptly, Meryall stood, swaying for a moment with the swiftness of her movement. Arledge regarded her calmly.

'I cannot do it, Arledge. Each time I try, I see that poor man, frightened and alone in the sheriff's cells.' Her voice was tight and low as she looked down at Arledge, who remained seated, staring into the flames, a slight smile on his lips.

'You are allowing yourself to be distracted, Meryall, by something that does not concern you. Dye will investigate and if the man is innocent, he need have nothing to fear.'

Meryall snorted. 'Nothing to fear other than perishing alone and in distress in her cells, you mean?'

Arledge turned his gaze on her, his eyes flinty. 'Fujikawa will tend to him. Dye will do her job. You should do yours and remember your purpose here.'

Meryall's chest contracted with anger. 'You seek to teach me to heal, yet you bid me to do nothing to help the one person who truly needs my help?' She shook her head. 'Clearly I can expect no support here.' She strode from the room, slamming the door behind her.

Meryall went to her room and pulled a quill and ink from her pack, scribbling a note on a scrap of parchment and sealing it hurriedly, marking Madoc's name on the outside.

She put on her shawl and cloak and stepped out into the snowy lane. The cold air was sobering. It kissed her hot cheeks and calmed her as she walked. By the time she had reached the village, she was almost recovered from her fit of temper, but she remained resolute. She paid a boy at the inn to take her message, giving him an extra coin to buy a warm meal at the inn before the return journey.

All she could do now was to await the reply.

Meryall walked back to Arledge's house, her feet sliding away from her at every other step. The snow in the lane had turned from slush back to ice as the cold set in again, making close attention to her footing necessary. She carried a basket of goods – feeling uneasy about the anger she had directed towards Arledge, Meryall had determined that she would make a start on the Samhain celebrations for him. She had collected oats and treacle to make the oatcakes that Arledge was to bless, for the mummers to hand out to the crowds at the bonfire that night, and had purchased red and green ribbons to decorate their hats and to tie as streamers on the branches that would decorate the threshold of the house.

Alys was in the kitchen when she arrived and eagerly took the heavy basket from Meryall, laying out the ingredients for the cakes. Meryall washed her hands in the icy water of the pump outside and went to assist Alys in mixing and forming the cakes in big batches. They went into the stove one after the other and would do for the rest of the day, until there were enough cakes to feed all of the village. Arledge emerged from his study and joined them, blessing the cakes as they came out of the oven and sprinkling them with a pinch of spice and a drizzle of honey to bring warmth and plenty to the revellers. It was afternoon when they stopped and the day was drawing in. Meryall and Alys packed bottles of mead and ale into baskets.

Alys went to the porch and peered down the lane. Meryall stood at her side, looking out into the darkness. In the cold air she could trace the smell of smoke. There were the first pricks of light bobbing along the lane – the occupants of the farms and houses were beginning their parade into the village square with lanterns and torches held aloft to light their way. They put on their boots and warmest cloaks and mittens and lit their own lanterns. Arledge had a lantern affixed to a tall pole carved with ivy leaves and the faces of the gods and goddesses. Alys and Meryall had tied ribbons to the pole and they streamed in the cold air as they waited for the column of people to reach them. Meryall heard voices raised in song and the tramp of many feet on the frozen ground as they drew closer. The group stopped at the gate to Arledge's house.

Arledge stepped out of the porch, holding the lantern high. He was wearing a tall black hat, with red ribbons and a long crow's feather in the brim. His white hair shone and his eyes blazed. The crowd grew quiet. Arledge raised his powerful, rich voice in a long, deep, ululating cry. As the note died away, he began an incantation, claiming the protection of the gods and goddesses of their land for the hard winter to come, honouring their dead and giving thanks for the blessings they had received this year. He poured mead on the ground and gave a final, triumphant cry. The crowd erupted into shouts of joy and the song restarted as they moved on along the road, with Arledge at the head of the parade.

Meryall followed, feeling the electric tingle of the air. Her mother had led the village's Samhain parade, but since her death, Meryall had agreed with Wyot that he had the superior standing and experience to lead the people of Thornton, although she provided the blessed cakes and mead.

They gathered people at each house they reached, until they entered the village square. The mummers were waiting in front of the bonfire. There were rowdy cheers and the stamping of heavy boots on the cobbled streets, almost cleared of snow by the heavy footfall of the parade.

The lead mummer, the blacksmith on non-feast days, raised his hand for silence. The mummers began their stylised play, miming the fight between good and evil, light and dark, as they had done for as long as anyone could remember. As ever, light triumphed over dark and the mummers lit the great fire to mark the end of their play and took the cakes, mead and ale from Alys and Meryall and began to hand them round, ensuring that every person ate and drank and received the blessings needed to help them through the hard months to come. The celebrations felt urgent; winter had arrived early and every piece of good luck would be needed for all to make it through the cold, dark months safely. The wild joy of the revellers carried a note of desperation. Each family knew that it was likely they would have to set fewer places at their table before the warmth of the sun returned.

A fiddler began to play and was joined by a flute. A fine alto voice rose over the noise of the crowd and Meryall looked round to see Dye, dressed in an ornate dress uniform, standing on a box, singing lustily. Meryall smiled and waved, but then the joy left her heart as she remembered that the stranger would be sitting alone in the cells, hearing the festivities around him but unable to join in. He, of all of them, was perhaps most in need of the blessings of the gods and goddesses.

Chapter 5

Meryall awoke with a start. The weak daylight was streaming into her room. It must be fully morning by now. She groaned. Her head ached from the ale and her throat was sore from too much talk and bonfire smoke. She sat on the edge of the bed and dragged her hands through her hair. Out of the thick blankets, it was cold in the little room and she shivered, wrapping her bed gown close to her. There was a soft knock at the door.

'Come in.' Meryall found it a strain to form the words. Alys came in, a steaming cup in her hands. Meryall sniffed. She could smell ginger. She took the cup from Alys with an attempt at a smile and sipped at it. It was a mixture of oats, a pinch of salt, ginger and honey, sieved to make a thickened drink. Alys picked up a bowl from the top of the stairs and brought it in. She dipped a folded rag into water infused with rosemary and thyme and put the cool compress on Meryall's forehead. Despite the cold of the room,

Meryall's face was flushed and warm. Alys winked at her, patted her shoulder and withdrew, leaving Meryall to feel the effect of her remedies.

Meryall drained her drink, lay back for five minutes, breathing the scent of the herbs, and then rose determinedly to her feet, ignoring the quiet murmurings of her stomach, which did not appear to approve of her movement.

Arledge was in the kitchen, looking calm and composed, eating a breakfast of salted fish and onions. Meryall's stomach again voiced its disapproval.

She greeted Arledge as cheerfully as possible and stepped out onto the porch, the cold, fresh air soothing her hot face. Today she must wait patiently for a reply to her message. In the meantime, she knew that she had much ground to regain with Arledge following their disagreement about the stranger.

In the kitchen, Alys was moving around tidying away dishes.

'Arledge is in the study,' she said as Meryall came in. 'He asked that you join him when you are ready.' Alys slid another cup of the oat and ginger drink over to her. Meryall dropped a kiss on Alys's cheek in thanks and took the cup through to the study.

Arledge was seated at his desk, a large volume open before him. He had put a second seat alongside his own. Meryall sat down next to him, placing her cup down well away from the books.

'There are few written records of our ways,' Arledge

said. 'Our traditions have been passed from one person to another, primarily, although some of us keep a note of our own remedies and charms. This text is my attempt to record some of what I know.' He looked at her, his eyes misty. 'I feared that you might not have the opportunity to learn all you have a right to, so Turi and I have been working on this project for many years.'

Meryall scrutinised the book. It was neatly written and the page before her was illustrated with drawings and symbols in coloured inks. A lump rose in her throat and she hastily turned away to pick up her cup, drawing her chair back a little from the table. She sipped her drink and swallowed hard to clear her throat.

'It is a valuable and beautiful work,' she said quietly.

Arledge smiled. 'I am going to see Fujikawa this morning, so may I leave you to examine the chapter on healing? It may help to consolidate our discussions. This afternoon, we will try a practical lesson once again.'

Meryall nodded her assent. 'Thank you, that would suit me well.'

Arledge chuckled. 'Indeed, healing is easier to focus on when one is not in need of healing oneself. By this afternoon, your head should have cleared.'

Meryall half laughed, half groaned. 'And what deal with the gods have you made that your head is so clear this morning? You took more ale than I!'

Arledge raised an eyebrow. 'That secret too you will

learn with time.' He patted her shoulder and turned to go, taking his cloak from a peg by the study door.

Meryall settled into her chair and turned her attention to the pages before her. She had begun to doze a little, soothed by Alys's drink and the warmth of the study, when the sound of footsteps approaching the porch roused her. She rubbed her eyes, glad that Arledge had not returned to find her asleep over his book.

She heard Alys greeting someone and frowned; the deep tones were not those of Arledge. Her heart skipped a beat. Meryall hurried into the hall. Alys was taking Madoc's cloak from him. He turned to Meryall, his arms outstretched. She rushed forward to kiss and embrace him, breathing in his clean smell. His clothes carried the scent of the herbs from his apothecary shop and his hair was filled with the smell of snow and fresh air.

'I had not expected you so soon!' Meryall said.

'I went to Wyot immediately upon receiving your message. He has provided me with a letter for his counterpart in this place, Sheriff Brereton, recommending that she accept your assistance in investigating the case of the stranger and citing the previous service you have done Wyot in similar cases.' Madoc took a scroll, sealed with Wyot's familiar mark, from his belt pouch.

Meryall ran her finger over the wax seal, her heart full. She sighed. 'I am afraid Arledge will not be pleased with me for doing this, Madoc.'

Madoc frowned. 'You have different opinions in the case?'

'Yes, Dye and Arledge are inclined to view the evidence of a body being found and the stranger having blood on his clothing as sufficient reason to mistrust the appearance of his innocence. I cannot argue with their logic, but I have looked within the man and can find no trace of aggression in him.'

Madoc was silent for a long moment before replying. 'I rather agree with their logic, but that does not mean that the case should not be thoroughly investigated. I believe you can help with the investigation – and I too am happy to assist by examining the body.'

'That is fair and just. I expected nothing less from you and Wyot. Thank you, my love.' Meryall kissed him, then pulled away. 'Arledge has gone into the village to Fujikawa. I must continue with my studies. I don't wish to displease him further.'

Alys appeared from the kitchen and took charge of Madoc, steering him to a chair by the fire and pulling cups and plates out of the dresser, fussing over him like a mother hen.

Meryall returned to the study and stoked the fire, the logs sending a shower of sparks into the air. She looked into the flames for a moment and felt a sudden pull. She would try to sit for the healing journey that Arledge had tried to support her with. She was in a better temper today and Arledge would be pleased if she could achieve it.

She looked around. Arledge had jars of herbs on a shelf above his desk. She selected a few sprigs of dried wormwood and cast them into the fire, breathing the strongly scented, aromatic smoke. Meryall seated herself comfortably and let her eyes rest on the flames. The fire danced and she looked far beyond the light, opening herself to the place beyond the physical realm.

Meryall started. The face of a man, dark-haired and sallow-skinned filled her vision. She recognised him at once. He was the man she had seen on the way to Samlesbury that spring, harassing the cunning woman Orlaith in the market. He had struck her as a hard and fanatical man. He pulled back, his face twisted with anger, and Meryall saw with a stab of fear that he had a knife in his hands. She was seeing him from the perspective of the person he was threatening, but she could not tell whose eyes she was seeing through, only the face of the man bearing down on her with the blade aimed at her heart.

Abruptly, Meryall was once again looking at the flames. Her heart pounded in her chest. She rubbed her eyes and ran her hands through her hair, disorientated for a moment by the intensity of the vision. It was not what she had sought and yet perhaps, on a level beyond that which she was conscious of, she had asked for this image.

She had been given an insight which might help to

prove the innocence of the stranger, for here was a man whose malevolence she had witnessed first-hand, shown to her with a knife in his hand and fury in his eyes.

Meryall paced the study. Madoc had joined her, having escaped the ministrations of Alys, who had seemed intent on feeding him enough food for his entire day's meals in one sitting, happy to have someone to test new recipes on as she cooked fruit for preserving and tended to a pudding for the evening meal. He was browsing Arledge's collection of books, picking up a volume on botany detailing rare and unusual plants. He had tried to distract Meryall from her pacing, showing her illustrations of faraway places they might visit some day in the large portfolios of paintings and drawings on Arledge's shelves, but she could not keep her mind even on such pleasant things. The image of the face of the man they had seen, with a knife in his hands in a woodland clearing, filled her mind's eye.

'Ah, Arledge, here you are!' they heard Alys exclaim. 'You have a—'

Meryall started to the door, then caught herself and sat down instead by the fireplace, restraining herself from crowding Arledge as he came into his house. Arledge walked into the study, the chill air clinging to him like an aura. Madoc stood and took Arledge's hand. Arledge greeted him with pleasure, but turned to look at Meryall with an eyebrow raised.

'I had not known I was to expect another visitor, Madoc, it is good to see you.'

'Meryall suggested that my experience in examining cadavers may be useful to Sheriff Brereton. I bring with me a letter from Wyot, recommending my services—' Madoc's eyes flitted to Meryall for a moment '—and vouching for the usefulness of Meryall's divination skills in matters such as this.'

Arledge sat down and steepled his fingers before him. 'Indeed. I see that Meryall's passion for justice will not allow her to leave the investigation alone.'

Meryall flushed, but meeting Arledge's eye, she saw amusement, rather than anger.

She smiled and took the seat opposite him, warming her hands at the fire as she gathered her thoughts. She had expected him to be furious with her for her interference and indeed she could not blame him; she had significantly exceeded her authority in Arledge's village, but he was a curious man, capable of generosity of spirit and great kindness. Perhaps his visit with Fujikawa had helped to soften his mood.

Cautiously, she told Arledge of the vision she had received. He nodded as he listened, a slight frown creasing his brow.

'Well, it appears that we must pay Dye a visit,' he said at last. 'But first, let us sit together and have a meal. You must be hungry, Madoc. And we may discuss how best to approach our discussion with Dye as we eat. What say you to renewing your acquaintance with Fujikawa?'

Madoc bowed. 'I would very much like to see him. I recently had a visit from Jura and have some curious herbs to show him.'

Alys packed a basket of provisions, sure that Fujikawa could not accommodate an impromptu meal for four people at short notice. Meryall added a bottle of parsnip wine from the stock she had brought with her and set out for the village with Madoc and Arledge in good spirits.

Meryall slipped her hand into Madoc's, glorying in the warmth of his skin against her own. It lent her the strength and reassurance that she sorely needed.

Chapter 6

The snow had thawed a little in the bright sunshine, but the harsh cold resisted the thaw and the melting snow reformed as glistening icicles hanging from the leaves and twigs and all along the edges of the roofs of the houses they passed.

Arledge and Madoc chatted about herbs and their mutual acquaintances as they walked, their voices ringing in the still air. Meryall was wrapped in her thoughts, a sense of hope for the stranger's acquittal swelling in her heart. She checked herself. Even if the stranger was innocent, a man had died a violent death and the perpetrator remained at large. There was cause for neither relief nor celebration. The features of the man in her vision rose in her mind's eye. She remembered her sense of his dark, fanatical energy when she had seen him harassing her fellow cunning woman, Orlaith, at her market stall in Samlesbury. Orlaith had told her he lived in an encampment of Christians, who lived in the woods nearby. What could have led him to kill and who was the victim who lay as yet unidentified in the sheriff's keep? Meryall's thoughts crowded in on her. She had intended that her season with Arledge be a time for learning and growth, away from her responsibilities as a cunning woman. She looked up at Madoc, his cheeks flushed with the cold and his eyes bright with animation as he talked. She still hoped that Arledge might allow Turi to look after Thornton Cleveleys for a while longer after she had finished her training with him so she and Madoc might take the journey together that they had abandoned after her mother's death. She had not broached the subject with him yet. It must wait until they were on a calmer footing with one another.

The windows of Fujikawa's apothecary shop were misted with condensation and lit by cheerful, ornate lanterns. The little bell on the door tinkled as they entered, bringing Fujikawa from the back room. He started with surprise at the sight of Madoc, coming forward to clasp his hand in welcome. He turned to Arledge and embraced him.

'I had not thought to see you for a second time today,' he said with pleasure. 'I am curious to hear what brings you all to my door, but first, let me offer you refreshments.'

Fujikawa was about to go into his store room when Arledge raised the basket and called to him to stop. Fujikawa looked into the basket and laughed.

'I should have known Alys would not send you

empty-handed,' he said wryly.

They sat down at a table hastily cleared of jars of herbs and weighing scales to the meal of cold pheasant, pear and honey pie, bannock bread, cheese and apples that Alys had packed for them.

Meryall briefed Fujikawa on the reason for their visit to the village. He nodded, eyeing her shrewdly from under his straight, dark brows as he poured small cups of parsnip wine for them all.

'I have seen the body already,' Fujikawa said to Madoc, 'but your knowledge of weapons wounds is much better than mine. Your examination might help us understand the type of knife used and the manner of the attack. I was able to say only that the knife strike was most likely to have been fatal, even if he had received help immediately.'

'I would be honoured to help. There are few areas in which your knowledge does not surpass mine. In fact, I was hoping to ask your opinion on some curious medicinal botanicals I have acquired.'

When they had eaten, they discussed how best to approach Dye. It was important that they were respectful of her authority and showed deference to her position in relation to their own. They agreed that it would be best to wait a little while longer as Dye would be eating her meal with her guards and would not appreciate the interruption. To make use of the time, Madoc pulled the packages of herbs his merchant friend Jura had given him from his belt pouch and he and

Fujikawa sat examining them and talking of their properties for some time, pinching and sniffing at the dried plants, sending unfamiliar, bitter, aromatic scents into the air like incense from a faraway land.

Meryall and Arledge sat together at the other end of the table talking of her mother, her training and avoiding talking about the stranger. Meryall was glad they were on better terms and did not want to endanger the peace between them by discussing the subject their opinions differed most on. There were difficult conversations to come, but she need not hurry them to the fore.

Sheriff Brereton's keep lay at the heart of the village. It was a heavy timbered structure, fortified with rough walls of red sandstone. A tall guard met them at the door of the great hall, bowing deferentially to Arledge. He ushered them to Dye, who was seated in a high-backed chair by the huge fireplace. A boar was roasting on a spit, bunches of herbs stuffed in slashes in the meat, filling the air with a tantalising, savoury scent. Meryall frowned. They had expected that Dye and her guards would have eaten by now, but at least it did not appear that they would be eating imminently and neither had they arrived during her meal. She took a deep breath to still her nerves.

The tables in the great hall were occupied by the men and women who served the sheriff. Laughter and cries of protest rang out from the scattered knots of dice games, and the clink of tankards of ale competed with the thin, earnest song of a bone flute.

Dye was dressed in a practical leather tunic and plain, rough cloth hose, her bronze hair braided tightly and tied with a strip of leather decorated with carved wooden beads. Meryall regarded her closely. She was a handsome woman, lean and of an imposing height; her skin, probably naturally fair, was freckled and tanned from an outdoor life. Her unusual amber eyes carried a touch of steel within their glance. She was not likely to be easily swayed by compassion, but would be won over by logic, Meryall calculated.

They were accommodated in chairs hurriedly arranged around Dye's seat. Their chairs were smaller than hers, making her height all the more intimidating, Meryall noted with amusement. She was sure this was not accidental.

Arledge introduced Madoc to Dye.

'Welcome, Madoc. I have heard you are considered a knowledgeable apothecary and bring experience from your travels abroad to your village,' she said with polished courtesy. 'What brings you to my hall?' Her eyes were keen, despite the mildness of her voice.

Madoc drew Wyot's scroll from his pouch. 'I bring word from my sheriff.' He handed it to her with a low bow.

Dye drew her knife from her belt and slid it under the seal. A servant brought cups of mead. Meryall sipped hers nervously, watching Dye's face as she read.

Dye's mouth twitched, almost imperceptibly. Meryall could not tell whether in a smirk of amusement or a grimace of annoyance.

Having finished the letter, Dye tossed it onto the table at her side. She looked from Meryall to Madoc coolly.

'I am honoured by my fellow sheriff's recommendations. If you believe you can assist my people in their investigations, by all means do so.' Dye paused, leaning slightly towards them. 'However, I must remind you that this is my jurisdiction and I will not tolerate any interference in my administration of justice.'

Meryall met her eye, feeling a jolt as the energy of their two strong wills locked against one another. She smiled, breaking eye contact and looking down in a show of obedience.

'Of course, Sheriff, we understand and are honoured by your confidence in us.'

'As well to begin at once whilst the evidence is fresh,' Dye said, rising to her feet and signalling to a servant, who ran to fetch horn lanterns. 'Let us view the body.'

The daylight was beginning to lose strength and within the confines of the stout stone wall, it was growing gloomy. In the windowless depths of the chambers below the great hall, it would be darker still.

The party followed Dye down into the basement. Meryall felt the air grow colder with each step they took into the depths of the keep. Their breath started to condense into clouds of steam before they were even halfway down and the cheerful fire of the great hall above them began to feel far away.

They walked through a long, narrow corridor, with thick doors spaced along it on either side. Torches hung in sconces along the stone walls, but the light of their lanterns was necessary to see the floor beneath their feet.

'I had not realised that the keep had stone passages below it,' Meryall said. 'Is this part of the building older than that above?'

'Yes, the cells and storerooms predate the timber keep. Our keep has seen turbulent times in the past and has been rebuilt on more than one occasion.' Dye stopped outside a door that was wider than the others and pulled a heavy bunch of keys from a chain at her waist.

The door creaked open and Meryall followed the others into a room with a low, arched ceiling. The room smelled of damp sandstone, but under that scent, even in the intense cold, was the faint, sweet, unmistakable stench of death. There were three rows of three long stone slabs. This chill, lonely place obviously functioned as the village's resting place for the dead, whilst they awaited burial. In this weather, there may be a need to hold the bodies here for some days until the ground became soft enough to dig. Meryall looked around. Five of the nine slabs were already occupied, the dead covered with long linen cloths.

A spasm of sadness shot through Meryall. It was the way of nature, but before the snow departed, it would carry away more of the old and the weak. The earliness of the snow had left many of the poorest people of the village unprepared, with inadequate clothing and insufficient stores of firewood and food.

Dye walked over to the far table at the back of the chamber and drew back the linen. Madoc and Fujikawa stepped forward. The servant held the lantern to light the torso of the body, illuminating the wound there. The cut appeared almost trivial but for the dried blood around it. It was a mere thumb's length wide, the edges a neat line. Meryall stood at the foot of the slab, watching them go about their work, murmuring hypotheses to one another about the angle, depth and placement of the wound. The light of the lantern threw the face of the dead man into shadow. She noted the tall, spare frame of the man and wondered who he was, who might be looking for their father, brother or husband, scouring the frozen landscape in search of him. There had been no word of any missing person, which made her wonder if he had been found far from his home.

At Madoc's request, the servant moved the lantern closer to the head to better shine the light on the upper chest. As the light shifted, the face was thrown into the beam of the lantern.

Shock surged through Meryall. Icy fingers gripped

her stomach and the floor seemed to move beneath her feet.

There, face set in a rictus of anger, lay the man who had been harassing Orlaith in the marketplace in Samlesbury – the man who had been holding the knife in her vision.

Chapter 7

Madoc stared at the face of the corpse and glanced towards Meryall. Her eyes were wide, fixed on the features before her. Madoc asked the servant to shift the light of the lantern again and the face was once more in darkness, breaking the spell Meryall had found herself under. She blinked and took a deep, shuddering breath to steady herself. Dye moved to her side.

'Being in the presence of the dead can be unnerving,' Dye said gently. 'May I ask the servant to take you back to the hall for a glass of whisky whilst the apothecaries finish their business here?'

Meryall shook her head. 'Thank you, it is not the sight of death that has put me out of spirits. However, I would speak to you, if you will return to the hall with me.'

Dye agreed graciously, taking one of the lanterns from a servant and guiding Meryall towards the door. Meryall looked back and caught Madoc's eye. He nodded, before returning to his work.

The warmth and light of the hall was dazzling after the darkness below the keep. Dye offered Meryall a seat by the fire, eyeing her pale features with a frown. She shouted for whisky to be brought and a servant hurried forward with a flask and cups.

Dye poured a measure and put it into Meryall's hands. 'Drink,' she said. 'You look near fainting.'

Meryall sipped at the whisky. The fiery warmth brought life back to her features.

'Thank you for your kindness,' Meryall said, hesitating over how to proceed.

Dye sat back in her chair, as if waiting for her to continue.

'Some time ago, Madoc and I travelled to Samlesbury. On our way there, we broke our journey in Dolphinholme and encountered an unpleasant man in the marketplace, a fanatic who was harassing the cunning woman of that place. Orlaith, the cunning woman, told us he was one of a group of Christians who lived in the woods thereabouts.' Meryall stopped and sipped at her whisky for a long moment, willing herself to proceed.

'I was granted a vision earlier today, although I had not sought it. In the vision, I saw the man from the marketplace with a knife raised, a look of fury upon his face, bearing down upon someone.'

Dye shifted in her seat, leaning towards Meryall, alert like a hound who has sighted its quarry.

Meryall sighed. 'I saw that face again just now. The body lying in the morgue is that of the Christian we saw in Dolphinholme.'

Dye sat back, her hands pressed together before her face. 'You are sure?'

Meryall nodded. 'Yes, his face is unmistakable. I believe Madoc recognised him too.'

Dye tapped her fingers on the table. 'The roads are clearer hereabouts, but conditions are still poor for a longer ride. We will assess the situation in the morning and, if possible, ride out to Dolphinholme in search of this camp.'

'May we return in the morning to visit the stranger? It would be wise to check on his condition,' Meryall said.

Dye gave her assent with a wave of her hand. 'Come when you will. Fujikawa visited yesterday to check the man over and found him to be somewhat recovered, although he states his memory has not returned to him. I find that to be overly convenient in these circumstances.'

Meryall looked at her hands and took a breath, deciding it was not worthwhile to reply. She was tired and disappointed. The day would hold nothing better for her than a hot meal and sleep and she longed for both.

The others entered the hall. Madoc's mouth was set in a grim line. Meryall avoided his eyes. Arledge stared at her for a long moment. Meryall guessed that Madoc had informed them of the identity of the victim.

She barely listened as they gave Dye their report, their voices drifting around her as she sat, impatient for the fresh air and liberty of the road.

At length, she raised her head to see that Arledge was holding his hand out to her, inviting her to rise. She took it and he squeezed her fingers gently, his pale blue eyes seeking hers. She avoided returning his glance and hurriedly bade Dye goodbye.

Outside, Meryall savoured the cold air on her face. Her eyes prickled with tears. Perhaps she had been wrong about the stranger; she could think of no other solution. Here was the man she had believed, hoped, to be guilty, disliking his appearance and his treatment of one of her own, lying dead with a wound in his chest. And here was the man she sought to defend, covered in blood and unable to account for his movements. No wonder Dye and Arledge had thought her a fool. A bitter, painful lump filled her throat and made it impossible to speak. The men around her diplomatically murmured amongst themselves, allowing her space to recover in peace.

Meryall tried to steady her breath, focusing on placing her feet on the road, the sweet air and the quiet cloak that the snow placed on the land.

Turning her thoughts to the stranger, she tried to recall how he had looked, how he had sounded, how her instincts had responded to him. She could still find no trace of the darkness or shadow she had seen in others who had done things such as this. She called to mind his boyish, freckled face and instinctively reached out to touch his spirit, her own spirit radiating out towards him through the golden light of the fading sun.

Meryall halted on the path, her eyes closed. She had a sudden sense of entrapment and pain and a burning heat filled her body, despite the cold. She felt the spirit of the stranger to be caged – not by the confines of his cell, but by something else. It was an eerie, ominous sensation that made her want to run away.

Arledge was at her side, sensing her distress. He reached out and touched her forehead, his own eyes closed as he sought to understand what had happened.

He removed his hand abruptly and put his hands on her shoulders, shaking them to bring her back to herself. She slumped for a moment before recovering.

'We must go back.' Meryall thought she had spoken, but realised that Arledge had said the words she had tried to speak. She looked at him gratefully. Something was very wrong with the stranger.

Fujikawa and Madoc turned with them without question and they retraced their steps to the keep.

Dye was surprised to see them, but agreed with a small shrug to allow them to see the stranger, sending a servant to guide them to his cell.

Once again, they walked through the dark, cold bowels of the keep, deeper this time, passing the large door of the morgue until they reached the end of the corridor. The servant unlocked the door to the cell and held it open for them to enter, closing it behind them. The room was small and icy cold, although Meryall noticed that the stranger had blankets wrapped around him. He appeared to be deep in sleep and did not stir as they entered.

Arledge stepped forward and touched the man's shoulder softly. He did not move. Arledge turned him onto his back. The stranger moaned quietly, but did not open his eyes. Arledge signalled Fujikawa to him. Fujikawa placed a hand on the stranger's forehead and frowned. He leaned down and pulled one of his eyes open, examining the pupil, then placed his hand at the stranger's throat, feeling for a pulse. Madoc joined them and they conferred quietly, Madoc too touching the stranger's face and neck. The stranger lay uncomplaining and seemingly unconscious of the scrutiny he was under throughout the examination. Meryall's heart beat hard in her chest.

Arledge called for the servant and sent him running for his sheriff.

Meryall caught at Arledge's arm as he moved back towards the stranger. 'How bad is it?'

Arledge sighed. 'Bad. He will not wake and burns with a savage fever. We fear for his life.'

'We must get him out of here,' Meryall said.

'I agree. We will take him to my house, where Fujikawa and Madoc can oversee his care.'

A rush of love and gratitude overwhelmed Meryall. 'And Alys will fuss over him and overfeed us all,' she said, life returning to her features at the prospect of removing the stranger from this dingy, cold place.

Dye agreed reluctantly for the stranger to be taken to Arledge's house, on condition that an armed guard go with them.

Before it seemed possible, they had arranged a litter to carry the stranger, borne on the shoulders of four strong guards, and were on the road.

Madoc walked on ahead of them to give Alys notice of their plans and to arrange a bed for the stranger before the fire in the kitchen, where he might easily be attended to.

Meryall looked at the still, flushed face of the stranger swaddled in blankets in the open litter like a babe. Where was this young man's mother? she wondered, for he must be known and loved somewhere.

Alys was waiting in the porch when they arrived and barked orders at the guards, who obeyed her with covert smiles, for they knew they would not leave without Alys pressing cakes into their hands, despite the fearsome manner she was currently displaying towards them.

The stranger settled in a hastily improvised bed and, all of the guards gone, with the exception of the man-at-arms who Alys insisted was seated out of the way in the nook by the back door, a plate of bread and meat occupying his attention, the house was at last calm.

Fujikawa and Madoc had prepared an infusion to be

gently dropped into the stranger's mouth every hour and had made cooling compresses, which Alys applied diligently to his forehead, hands and feet.

Meryall sat with Arledge in his study. Now, she knew, her training in the healing arts must begin.

Chapter 8

The intense cold had gone and the snow began to thaw. Meryall looked out from the porch, inspecting the road conditions. Dye and her guards should be able to take to the road today, in search of the name and family of the victim.

She returned to the kitchen. The scent of the juniper berries burned to dispel infection and the medicines Madoc and Fujikawa had brewed filled the air. All night, the stranger had lain in a burning fever, unwaking, his sleep punctuated by periods of murmuring and crying out. Fujikawa and Madoc had taken turns sitting up with him, administering willow bark and yarrow infusions and applying poultices of ginger to his feet. Madoc, taking the pre-dawn shift, had gone to bed to sleep for an hour or two, once the others were up.

Meryall had watched Arledge's contribution to the man's treatment intently. Arledge used fever stones – precious, pale pink stones he had received from a cunning woman whilst travelling in Scotland – to bless the water for the infusions and sat holding the stranger's hands, using power called down from the great goddess, mother of all, to feed strength into the man's weak body and chase the fever from his bones.

Meryall tried once again to find her connection to the power. Turning her mind within to still her thoughts, she found a quiet place in her centre, unaffected by the turbulence of her emotions. She allowed her spirit to flow out and around her, seeking the power Arledge had described to her. At first, all she could feel was the chaos of the spirits and movements of the people around her. She swatted away the distractions, looking on and on. A delicate golden thread lay at her feet. As she reached down and put her fingertips to it, she was surrounded by a powerful sensation of warmth and comfort and knew she had found what she sought. In a moment, her consciousness of success displaced her concentration and the thread was gone, leaving her cold and alone. Meryall sighed, then shook her head at herself, laughing. She had done it, if only for a second; she had found her connection.

Arledge was working on the stranger, his eyes closed, forehead creased with concentration. She watched, fascinated, as a dark, swirling mist rose out of the stranger's body, guided by Arledge's hands, and was sent rushing out of the room.

The stranger stirred, his eyelids fluttering. Fujikawa came forward with a bottle of lavender vinegar and placed it under the stranger's nostrils. The sharp scent seemed to bring him more to himself and he opened his eyes fully, blinking, unfocused at first, but appearing more lucid by the second. He smiled weakly and cleared his throat, trying to speak.

Arledge trickled a little water into his mouth to ease his throat. The stranger swallowed it and asked for more. A cup was brought to him and he was supported to sit up and drink.

Meryall's heart lifted. The fever had broken, he was out of danger.

Alys took her turn watching over the stranger whilst they ate their breakfast in Arledge's study so as not to disturb him. After a brief period of talk and sitting up, he had returned to a sleep that appeared so peaceful and restorative that they were all keen to ensure it continued.

Madoc had awoken and joined them. 'Has his memory returned to him?' he asked.

Arledge shook his head. 'No, I fear that the fever will not have helped his recovery in that respect. However, the old cunning ways spoke of a means of retrieving lost memories. I have never had need to try it myself. It requires someone with good dream walking skills, who has a bond of trust with the subject. What say you, Meryall? You have earned the man's trust.'

Meryall started in surprise. 'I have never heard of

such a ritual. How is it performed?'

Arledge refilled his mug with milk and sipped. 'It requires a journey, much like a dream walk, into a layer of consciousness beyond the waking mind. You must find your way into the stranger's memory and help him recover what has been lost. You act as a curator of his memories, helping him to find and understand them. I have accounts of it in one of the books of shadows I received from an elder. Let us spend the morning reviewing them together. This afternoon, we will attempt the ritual.'

A thrill of anxiety swept through Meryall. She had never tried anything of this nature.

'Are there risks involved in the ritual?' she asked Arledge, looking earnestly into his eyes.

Arledge shrugged. 'There are always risks in our work, Meryall, but the risks are reduced by preparation and carefulness.'

Meryall picked at a loose thread on her shawl. 'Is there a chance I could damage his memory further, if I am not successful?'

Arledge rose and stood before the fire, warming his long, slender hands.

'You do not have to undertake this task if you do not wish to. I can only suggest that we review all of the information we can command before you decide against it.'

'I cannot think of an alternative,' Meryall replied. 'The roads will be clear soon and Dye will be travelling to Dolphinholme in search of answers about the victim. We must work to bring the stranger's memory back so he may be fit to answer his accusers. I will do all I can.'

Arledge smiled.

Fujikawa and Madoc passed their morning in the kitchen, caring for the stranger and exchanging talk of their travels and remedies.

Arledge and Meryall took seats before the fire in the study, the table between them scattered with books. Meryall looked at the volume open before her. It was the book of shadows of a long-dead, great cunning woman, Frida Winrow of Pendle. Arledge had known her in his youth and spent time under her tutelage. The book was covered in green leather, a pattern of ivy leaves tooled into the leather and highlighted with white pigment. Her writing had been neat and meticulous and the contents of the book were carefully detailed and categorised, the pages numbered for ease of reference. Meryall chuckled. Her mother's book of shadows was covered with little sketches of flowers and snatches of charms. It was a beautiful object, but difficult to navigate for anyone other than the author, unlike Frida's book.

Meryall ran her fingers over the cover and felt a shiver, as if someone's breath had raised the hairs on the back of her neck. She sniffed, catching the smell of linden flowers. She looked around, seeking the source of the scent. Madoc often made a tisane of linden flowers, but he was nowhere to be seen. She lifted the book to her nose, wondering if Frida had placed dried flowers between the pages on some long-ago summer's day. She heard a low, breathy chuckle from behind her.

'Alys?' Meryall turned in her seat. Nothing. Arledge was looking at her, his eyebrow quirked.

'Was it the scent of linden, or did she poke you in the back?' he said.

'Linden,' Meryall replied. 'Ow!' she exclaimed, feeling a sharp prod at her shoulder. She stood up, looking around the room, puzzled.

'It is one of Frida's favourite tricks,' Arledge said. 'I did not know you had the talent for object magic.'

'I don't, although my mother could hold any object and connect with its owner, living or dead,' Meryall replied, still looking confused.

Arledge beamed. 'Well, this is a good sign that your powers are maturing. It is timely, too. Frida will help guide you to the information you need.'

Meryall closed her eyes and tracked the sensations around her. She could feel an aura near her left shoulder, a warm pressure that was pleasant and reassuring. The scent of linden flowers lingered in the air, bringing memories of honey and summer grasses, despite the snowy weather. She lifted Frida's book and let her fingers find their way through the pages, stopping intuitively and laying the book on her lap. She opened her eyes and looked down at the page. It was illustrated with a line drawing in a tawny oak, faded with age, of a crow's feather and a hawthorn leaf. Meryall read, the words filling her mind in a voice that was not her own, a humorous, sharp voice that seemed to be halfway between scolding and laughing at any given moment.

The ills of the Marlor girl continue – she was gravely injured after the May Day revels and it is clear that the harm was done to her intentionally, but she cannot recall who the culprit was. I have tried to restore her memory with every herb I can think of that might serve the purpose, yet she does not improve. Consequently, another method must be tried. The child has faith in me, so I will try to walk alongside her, in the plane between waking and sleeping, to find the memories she cannot. It is not something I have attempted above once or twice before, but I am confident it can be done in this case.

Meryall turned the page. The next entry was dated two days later.

Little Rosa Marlor has recovered her memory and her assailant has been brought to justice. We spent a long night together to retrace the memories that had sunk to the bottom of her mind, like pebbles into the mud at the bottom of a clear, cool stream. It is not always well to recover memories. Often, deeds are forgotten for a reason and it can be detrimental to bring them back to the light; however in this case, we were so concerned for the safety of the girls of the village that the risk had to be taken. Rosa, being the brave girl she is, was as intent on finding the knave as we were.

I gathered all of the supplies I would need and took them to the Marlor cottage. We both drank of the tea I use for dream walking and I arranged the protective herbs around us and burned wormwood in the hearth. Rosa lay down and I watched over her until I could be sure she was sleeping deeply. The trick to journeying into the memory is to find the space between the sleeping mind and the conscious one. I took her hands and whispered into her ear what it was that she was to remember, describing to her the last thing she had been able to tell us before her memory was disrupted. Then I stepped into her dream state and guided her back through her broken memories. There was a great wall of fog, her mind's protection from the pain of her experience, but when we were able to break through this, the face of her attacker rose through the layers of her memory and was shown to us as clearly as one's own face in the mirror.

Meryall sat back, the book in her lap. Frida made it sound a simple task, yet it had taken Meryall years to master dream walking. This journeying to a space between waking and dreaming was new to her. She ran her fingers over her hair, absently tucking escaped strands of hair back into her braid. What if, even if she could do it, she caused permanent damage to the stranger by forcing him to retrieve memories that would be better left undisturbed? He was in a delicate state of health.

Meryall placed the book on the table and stood, stretching. 'Would you like a cup of warmed mead?' she asked Arledge.

'Yes, or better still, ask Alys to make us a jug of lambswool.'

Meryall grinned. She was fond of lambswool and knew Alys was proud of her own recipe, which was unfailingly delicious, the apples fluffy and the sweetness and spice perfectly balanced.

Alys was in the kitchen, busy scouring pots with sand, a huge pot of broth simmering over the fire. Madoc and Fujikawa had gone to Fujikawa's shop to look through his stores and consult his books in search of remedies for the stranger.

'Alys, would you please help me make a jug of lambswool? Arledge has a fancy for some.'

Alys readily assented, but waved Meryall's offered help away, instructing her to sit before the fire instead whilst she worked.

Meryall took her seat next to the stranger. He had been dozing, though he opened his eyes when she sat down, blinking sleepily, yet smiling a little.

'It is good to see you,' he said, his voice still hoarse.

Meryall smiled back at him, searching his open, freckled face once again for indications he could have done that of which he was accused.

'I have been consulting with Arledge,' she said. 'We believe it may be possible I can help you recover your memory.'

The stranger half sat up, his eyes alight.

'You truly think so? It is all I could ask for,' he said, his breath coming fast and shallow.

Meryall gently touched his shoulder. 'Calm yourself, you are not strong enough for such excitement as yet.'

He lay back down, his eyes remaining fixed on her face, waiting for her answer.

'Yes, it may be possible. The old cunning folk spoke of it, but they also spoke of the risks of such a ritual—'

'I do not care,' the stranger interrupted. 'As long as the risks are to myself, I mean,' he said after a moment. 'Please, Meryall, if it does not place you in danger, I care not for the risk to myself. I cannot stand the torment of not knowing myself, nor what I may have done.'

Meryall sighed. 'Of course. Now, rest and let Alys feed you, for we will both need our strength tonight.'

Meryall hoped that she was doing the right thing.

Chapter 9

Meryall had gathered her herbs around her and brewed the tisane she used for dream walking. The garlands of protective herbs were laid and the bundle of wormwood lay ready to be cast into the fire. Arledge was across the kitchen table from her, watching her preparations.

Madoc and Fujikawa had retired to Fujikawa's house for the night to give them the space they needed for the ritual. Alys had left a basket for them packed with provisions fit for a small army and had fed Dye's guard, giving him fierce injunctions to stay out of her master's way. The fellow had been relegated to the rear woodshed, where he had been furnished with blankets, a small brazier of coals, a flask of broth and a flagon of ale. Satisfied that he could justly say none may pass out of the house without him seeing, due to the commanding position of the shed, he was quite content.

Meryall picked at the wormwood, pulling at the red thread that bound the bundle tightly together.

'Are you ready?' Arledge asked, his voice soft. The stranger had drunk his cup of tisane and had fallen into a sweet, peaceful sleep.

Meryall bit her lip. 'Arledge—' she paused '—why are you supporting me to help the stranger? I know you mistrusted the appearance of his goodness.'

Arledge traced the grain of the oak table with his fingers. 'I am helping you because I believe in the truth. I agree with you that this stranger does not carry an air of guilt or malice, but as we have discussed that does not mean he did not commit an act of savagery, perhaps in self-defence. This is our best opportunity to be sure of what happened.'

Meryall reached across and squeezed his hand. 'I am sorry. I have been arrogant and wilful. It was disrespectful of me to write to Madoc and Wyot without your blessing.'

Arledge chuckled. 'No apology is necessary, you followed your instincts and acted on your sense of justice.' He looked over at the stranger. 'I believe now would be a good time to make a start.'

Meryall stood and cast the wormwood into the fire. She tied a red thread to her wrist, connecting the other end to the stranger's wrist and tying it off on the pearwood chair she sat in at his side.

She clasped his hand and closed her eyes, the familiar sensation of her aura billowing outward into the space around them, flowing over the stranger's aura and mingling with his energy. She felt the deep, steady pulse of Arledge's energy as he sat watching over them at the table. She paused for a moment. There was another energy there too, fainter, but lively and bright. She bit her lip, tears of gratitude filling her eyes for the kindness of those around her. Frida's aura tingled around her as the old woman's spirit watched over them, curious and bustling, but protective.

Meryall sat for a long time, her anxiety about what she might see in the stranger's memories and her fear of hurting him anchoring her to her body. She slowed her breathing until she was almost at the point of sleep, her body heavy in the chair, then stepped into the stranger's space, feeling the subtle push of his energy, like running her hand through cool water, as she moved into his dream plane, whispering to him, to remind him of where they needed to go.

She was in a forest. The stranger stood before her. They were in a clearing. Meryall cast her eyes around. She could find no familiar landmarks to indicate where they were.

The stranger seemed to be waiting for someone. She heard the sound of footsteps moving through the forest towards them and turned, looking to see who was approaching them. A thick grey mist descended upon the clearing. The stranger turned towards her, his face filled with panic.

'Run!' he cried.

Meryall was thrown backwards with force. She awoke with a jerk, almost falling from her chair, her heart pounding in her chest. The thread around her wrist had snapped with her movement. She looked down at the stranger. Still he slept on, although he moved fitfully now, a slight frown on his face.

Meryall looked up at Arledge, who was hurrying towards her. She shook her head, unable to speak. He was there in a moment, his arm around her shoulder, stroking her hair from her face with his cool hands. He moved away and returned with a cup of warm, strong, spiced mead. Meryall took the cup, her hands shaking.

Arledge turned his attention to the stranger, feeling his pulse and placing his hand on his forehead.

'He is well. His temperature is raised a little and his pulse somewhat quick, but his fever has not returned. We should let him sleep now.'

Arledge pulled Meryall to her feet and steered her into the study, putting her into his chair, arranging her shawl around her shoulders and placing a stool under her feet.

He went into the kitchen and returned with the basket of provisions Alys had left.

Meryall smiled weakly. 'I am not sure I can eat, Arledge.'

Arledge shook his head. 'You must eat. Care for the body is the best remedy for the spirit.'

She allowed Arledge to put a plate before her. He had arranged slices of cold meat, cheese and oatcakes and was refilling her cup. She ate obediently, but could scarcely swallow. She had failed. And until the stranger woke, who knew what damage she had caused.

Meryall's sleep was punctuated by brief flashes of the stranger's terrified face and the mist closing in on them. She woke, sweating, in spite of the cold, in the early hours of the morning. She rose and went to the window, pulling back the heavy curtain and opening the wooden shutters. It was still dark outside, but the fading moonlight reflected off the snow and the pale dawn light filtered along the edge of the horizon. The world below her was silent under the crisp, still air. The scent of snow filled the room and Meryall revelled in the freshness, even as she shivered at the icy breeze.

She stayed at the window for a while longer before closing the shutter and curtains and pulling on her chemise and gown. Meryall put on a pair of thick woollen stockings and the Spanish leather boots Madoc had given her. She grimaced as she remembered that she still had not spoken to Arledge to ask if Turi would stay on at Horn Cottage for a few months longer so she and Madoc could travel together. She wanted to assure Madoc that all was confirmed before he returned to Thornton Cleveleys, but there had not been a good time to talk to Arledge, in the midst of all that had been happening. Meryall shrugged. Again, today was unlikely to be a day when such a conversation was possible.

Meryall trod as softly as she could down the oak stairs, trying to recall which treads creaked. The kitchen was quiet. It was too early even for Alys to have arrived. Meryall looked into the nook by the fire that held the stranger. He lay sleeping, his face peaceful, his hair curling on his brow like a child's.

Meryall turned away. Alys had left water ready in the kettle. Meryall set it to boil and went into Arledge's study to select herbs for a tisane. She chose dried elderberries, which were nourishing and comforting to the body. Meryall was glad that this year's elderberries were all picked and preserved or set to dry before the snow had come in. Her own stores were filled with bottles of elderberry elixir and young elderberry wine, maturing in the dark of her pantry. After some thought, Meryall also selected elfdock root. Elfdock, a tall, handsome plant, was useful in reducing fever, but was also a good general tonic which gave strength to overtaxed minds and bodies. The brew would be well-suited to the needs of all of those gathered in Arledge's house this morning.

The kettle was beginning to steam when she returned to the kitchen. Meryall added honey to the pot to balance out the bitterness of the elfdock and the tanginess of the elderberries and poured over the water. The rich scent of autumn filled her nose and the steam kissed her face, bringing roses to her cheeks. She stood and breathed in the steam for a moment, enjoying the warmth and perfume of the tisane, before putting the lid on tightly to prevent the beneficial properties escaping with the steam.

She put the pot on the table and set out cups. The stranger rubbed his eyes and stretched.

'I trust you slept well,' she said.

'I did,' he replied.

'Do you remember anything at all from the ritual?' Meryall asked.

The stranger shook his head. 'I have a vague recollection of unsettling dreams, but nothing specific, just an impression of feeling afraid.'

Meryall nodded. 'That is to be expected.' She sighed. 'I am sorry that we did not succeed in returning your memories to you.'

He bowed his head. 'We may succeed yet, we suffered no ills and we may try again.'

Meryall smiled. 'You are right. I am glad to find you unharmed. I was concerned that you may have been injured, or your fever provoked by our work.'

The stranger sat up straight and gave a brave smile.

'I am quite well, as you can see,' he replied.

The back door opened and Alys entered, a basket on her arm, wrapped in a cloak and a thick shawl against the cold.

'I have made us a tisane, Alys,' Meryall said, going over to hug her and take her basket so she could remove her heavy layers.

'Excellent!' said Arledge, who had entered the kitchen without Meryall hearing. He went to the table and filled the cups, sniffing appreciatively. 'Elderberry and elfdock,' he said. 'A good choice for our patient and good for all of us in this cold weather.'

He took a cup over to the stranger, peering into his eyes and feeling his pulse. Arledge gave a nod of satisfaction before handing the stranger his cup, then helped him to sit up a little, propped up by a rolled blanket.

'I have an idea,' Meryall said, as Arledge took a seat at the table next to her. 'The stranger's last memory is of being at the Sunn Inn in Samlesbury. We know Eda, innkeeper of that place, well and I am sure we will receive a warm welcome. Being there may help the stranger regain his memory. Eda may recognise him and be able to tell us more about what brought him to her inn.'

Arledge regarded the stranger. 'He is still weak, but he may make the journey, well wrapped and fortified with tonics and food to keep him warm and well. We will need to borrow horses from Dye. The roads are looking clearer and the cold will be less intense tonight. We should be able to make the journey safely, if we start early tomorrow.'

The stranger sat up straight, listening intently to their conversation. 'I would like very much to go,' he said.

'Do you think Dye will allow it?' Meryall asked Arledge.

'She will need persuading and likely will want to

send a guard with us, but I cannot see her objecting. The stranger is still weak and unlikely to run far, even if he tried to escape, and assistance in resolving the case will be welcome,' Arledge replied, rising from the table. 'Let us go to the sheriff's keep now. We will look in on Fujikawa and Madoc on the way there.'

Alys insisted they ate fresh bannock bread and eggs before they left, swathed in their layers of warm clothing.

The air outside was crisp, but the sun was stronger and although the snow still lay on the fields and trees, the day felt more like the autumn day it was. Meryall tilted back her face, enjoying the warmth of the sunshine.

The road was almost clear, the traffic of many feet and horses having mashed the snow into mush and the mush was beginning to melt.

Meryall wondered how Turi was getting on with caring for Horn Cottage and the village. In Madoc's absence, he would be receiving extra visitors, looking for herbal remedies and charms for colds and sore throats, aches and pains. Arledge had a keen knowledge of herbs and had taught his apprentice well.

Meryall wondered who might take care of Madoc's shop in his absence, if they were to travel. There was a group of scholars living in the nearby village of Byspham, who had a keen interest in herbs, growing many varieties in their gardens. Madoc was on excellent terms with them and one of them might be persuaded to take care of the shop and serve the people of the village whilst they were gone.

Madoc and Fujikawa were sitting eating their breakfast when they arrived. Arledge told them of their plan.

Madoc and Fujikawa looked at each other uneasily.

'I am not sure it is wise to move the stranger so soon after his illness. He remains weak and it is a long ride to Samlesbury, it is near twenty miles,' Fujikawa said.

'We will break the journey in Werlows. I know the cunning woman there and she will happily accommodate us, allowing us to rest,' Arledge said.

'If you insist on going, I will come with you, in case the stranger requires treatment,' Fujikawa said, his usually calm face set in firm lines.

'That would be wise,' Arledge said smoothly, the trace of a smile on his lips.

Madoc drew Meryall aside. 'I must go home today. I do not want to trespass on Turi's goodness for too long.'

Meryall nodded. 'I thought that would be the case.' She put her arms around his waist, resting her head on his shoulder. 'I will write to you when we get home.'

Madoc grinned. 'Wyot will be waiting for an update, no less than I will.'

Madoc went to put together his things whilst Fujikawa cleared the table. They set out together, Madoc turning to take the road to Thornton Cleveleys, as the rest of the party continued on to the keep.

Meryall watched him go with a heavy heart. It had been comforting to have him nearby. She had not realised how much she missed him.

Chapter 10

Dye's stables had supplied them with an assortment of mounts. Dye's man-at-arms had been relieved of his duty and replaced with another, Hew, who was to accompany them to Samlesbury.

Meryall was to be mounted on a neat chestnut fell pony with tufted fetlocks and a shining mane. She stroked his neck. She liked the solid, peaceable ponies. Wyot was well known as a breeder of fell ponies and she wondered if hers had come from Wyot's stock.

Arledge was also allocated a fell pony; his was black with a white star on his forehead. Hew and the stranger were mounted on larger mouse-coloured steeds. Meryall suspected they were of highland stock. The ponies of the highlands were renowned for their strength and hardiness, their home in the wild climates of remote parts of Scotland giving them endurance and patience.

Hew had fashioned a support for the stranger's

saddle, attaching an old chair back with curved arms to the rear and adding a rope strap to prevent the stranger from falling if he fell asleep or lost consciousness. The stranger's pony was roped to Hew's mount so he need not have the trouble of holding the reins and directing his pony.

Meryall watched Hew making the preparations for the journey with appreciation. His thoroughness and thoughtfulness impressed her and gave her a sense of his disposition. She was glad that Dye had chosen him to go with them.

The stranger settled into his saddle, his blankets tented around him and the rope strap secured around him. He seemed in good spirits and Meryall hoped that the air and light would do him good. Today was milder and the sun was making a valiant effort to chase away the remaining snow, but there was still a bite to the wind.

The party mounted and bid Dye farewell. The first part of their journey took them further inland. The thin, narrow road led across the moors. The snow had started to clear, leaving island grasses in the midst of the white. Birdsong filled the air. The birds would be hungry, after the sudden snow, which must have robbed them of their food.

They rode in single file on the narrow track, with Hew at the front of their party, leading the stranger's pony as the stranger dozed, lulled by the steady movements of his mount beneath him.

They paused after an hour or so on the road, mindful of the stranger's still delicate health. Hew helped him to dismount so he could stretch his legs.

Alys had packed a flask of mulled wine, tightly wrapped in a woollen shawl. Meryall took it from her pack and filled the wooden cups Alys had added to her pack, handing them round. The warmth and scent of spice brought cheer to the party and colour to their faces. Arledge passed round a package of honey cakes that had been put into his care by Alys, keen to fill their saddlebags with as much food as they could carry between them, despite being reassured that they would reach Werlows in plenty of time for their evening meal and could reprovision there.

Meryall stepped off the path to fill their cups with snow to clean them before putting them back in her pack. She bent to scoop snow into the first cup. A movement caught her eye. A hare hunched low in a patch of heather, his long, black-tipped ears lying along his back, twitching softly as he looked back at her. Meryall blinked in surprise. She stood up carefully, not wishing to startle him, but at her movement, he leapt with liquid grace into a bounding run across the moor and was soon out of sight. The stranger was standing at the side of the road a short distance from Meryall, leaning against a stone waymarker. She caught his eye. He had seen it too.

Fujikawa came over to the stranger and examined him briefly, nodding in satisfaction and giving him a spoonful of herbal tincture.

They remounted and continued on the road. They had just five miles left until they arrived at Werlows and ample time, so they walked their horses at a leisurely pace, making the journey as easy as possible for the stranger. Meryall noticed with pleasure that he was looking more alert and the fresh air had brought colour to his face, which had been left pale by the fever.

The group turned into the road to Inskip. A woman with long grey hair stood waiting at the gate to a thatched cottage. Arledge raised his hand in greeting.

She walked down the lane towards them. Arledge dismounted to meet her.

'Bridie, thank you for agreeing to accommodate us,' he said, pressing the woman's hands warmly.

Meryall smiled to herself. Of course, Arledge would have journeyed to speak to Bridie before they set out.

Bridie turned to look at them with sharp brown eyes. 'You are welcome in my home, please come in.' She opened the gate for them and guided them to a barn at the rear of the cottage. 'Your ponies will be comfortable here. I have put out fresh water and feed for them.'

Hew stayed behind to unsaddle and rub the horses down, waving away offered help from the others.

Bridie's kitchen was filled with the delicious scents of cooking. Meryall sniffed deeply. She could trace the wholesome smell of oat bread and there was a pot of broth simmering, which carried the aroma of garlic, thyme and onions.

She showed them where they would be sleeping – Meryall had a narrow cot in the attic, Arledge and Fujikawa had a bed in the second bedroom and Hew and the stranger were to sleep by the fire in the kitchen, to keep the stranger well guarded from the cold.

The cottage was cosy and welcoming. Bridie was a fine craftswoman and her wood carvings graced the furniture and her cheerful hand-dyed and woven blankets made the beds look warm and comforting.

Bridie seated them at the long scrubbed wood table, putting out drinks of warm milk with honey and a sprinkle of ground wood avens root, with its soft, aromatic flavour.

Bridie listened to Arledge and Meryall explaining the reason for their journey whilst she moved around the kitchen, stirring, tasting and taking out bowls, knives and spoons for their meal.

'Have you spoken to Orlaith, cunning woman of Dolphinholme?' Bridie asked Meryall as they sat down to eat.

Meryall shook her head, her mouth full of oat bread. 'No,' she said, swallowing her bread. 'I have not dream walked to her as yet.'

Bridie studied Meryall. 'You have not yet learned to project yourself in your waking form?'

Meryall blushed. 'I have limited experience with making a connection when both parties are awake, but hope that my time with Arledge will remedy that.'

'No time like the present,' Bridie said with a broad

grin. 'Shall we try after dinner? Her knowledge will be useful to you in your quest for information about this stranger of yours.'

They looked over to where Fujikawa and the stranger were talking quietly at the other end of the table. Fujikawa appeared to have taken a liking to the young man, who was interested in plants and in Fujikawa's travels and homeland. Meryall stretched. She was tired and had hoped for an easy evening of mead and talk, but Bridie was right, Orlaith's information would be useful to them and it would be easier for her to reach Orlaith from here, as they were closer to Dolphinholme than they would be at Arledge's house or the Sunn Inn.

After dinner, Bridie and Arledge withdrew from the kitchen with Meryall, leaving Fujikawa and the stranger to the fire and their chatter, and went into the parlour, which was full of handsome furniture and the walls were adorned with tapestries of her own making. Bridie lit beeswax candles. The flickering golden light sent the woven gods and goddesses dancing across the wool, surrounded by sacred owls, stags and oak leaves.

Bridie struck her flint until a spark leapt into the kindling. A fire was soon blazing in the hearth. It was a beautiful room, Bridie was undoubtedly skilled, but more than that, her artistry brought a sense of power and safety to the room, with the figures around the room seeming joyful and strong.

Bridie and Arledge agreed with a subtle look between them that Bridie would guide Meryall.

She took a seat on a rug by the fire and gently pulled Meryall's hand to invite her to sit before her. Bridie took a bunch of herbs from her apron pocket and cast the dried leaves and stems into the fire. Meryall sniffed. The familiar scent of sage filled the air.

Bridie took Meryall's hands in her own small, strong ones.

'Close your eyes,' she said. 'Call to mind the image of Orlaith, bringing as much detail as you can about her appearance and energy.'

Meryall focused on Orlaith as she had seen her in Dolphinholme, her tall back straight and narrow, high colour in her cheeks and shining golden hair, touched with grey at the temples.

'Ask permission of her essence to allow you to reach out to her,' Bridie said, her voice sounding far away to Meryall.

Meryall sent out a shaft of light from her heart, a pure beacon beaming towards Orlaith.

In a moment, she stood in a light-filled space. She blinked, the brilliance of her surroundings dazzling. Orlaith stood before her, her hands on her hips and a faint frown on her attractive face.

'I remember you, you are a cunning woman, but I cannot recall your name,' she said.

Meryall bowed. 'Thank you, Orlaith, for heeding my call. I am Meryall, cunning woman of Thornton Cleveleys. I have come to ask for your help in a matter of grave importance.'

Orlaith bowed in return. 'Then proceed, Meryall of Thornton Cleveleys. I am at your service.'

'The man in black we saw in Dolphinholme that day harassing you – he has been found dead near Poltun. What can you tell me about him?'

Orlaith whistled in surprise. 'Dead? Well, he was an unpleasant man, yet I am sad to hear of the death of a man still in his prime. What happened?'

Meryall shrugged. 'We cannot be sure, but he met a violent end.'

'He was not a popular man,' Orlaith said, her face deep in thought as she searched her memory. 'His name was Michael Blackmantle. The Christian camp where he lived grew tired of his fanaticism and he relocated to another camp near Samlesbury, I believe. I have not seen him since he left. The people of his camp did not appear sorry that he had gone.'

'I wonder if he was better liked at his new camp,' Meryall said thoughtfully.

'That I do not know,' Orlaith replied. 'He was certainly a man who believed in his mission, despite few of his fellows agreeing with his position.'

Meryall thanked Orlaith and withdrew, pulling her consciousness back to the warmth of the fire and the feel of Bridie's hands on her own.

She looked round, seeking Arledge's eye. 'We are in luck – we have both a name and a last known dwelling for our dead man, which happens to be close to Samlesbury.'

They passed the evening in talk of Michael Blackmantle and the possible motives for his killing. They could not think how the stranger could be connected to him, but Arledge cautioned Meryall to keep an open mind with regards to the case.

Meryall slept well; her dreams were less turbulent than in recent nights and the peacefulness of Bridie's house soothed her. She woke early, whilst it was still dark, and lay in the warmth of her bed for a time, enjoying the quiet, knowing their day would be busy and demanding.

She went downstairs, her bare feet quiet on the well-worn wooden boards of the stairs. Fujikawa was pottering around the kitchen. He looked up as she opened the door, smiling in greeting, before winking and putting his finger to his lips. Meryall crept forward. The stranger lay asleep on his straw mattress, wrapped in Bridie's colourful blankets. His features were peaceful and still.

Fujikawa poured a cup of warm, spiced milk, thickened with ground oats and pushed it across the table to Meryall. She sipped gratefully at her drink, shifting the cup between her hands to warm them.

'What do you make of our stranger?' she asked him.

Fujikawa sat down next to her. 'He is intelligent and sweet-natured,' he said.

'So, you do not believe him guilty of killing this man, this Michael Blackmantle?'

'I did not say that,' Fujikawa replied. 'Although I believe it to be unlikely that he intended to kill him, if he was involved in the death.'

Meryall sighed. 'You are right. I suppose the single wound suggests that whoever killed Blackmantle did not kill him in a frenzy, but rather in a desperate moment of violence.'

Fujikawa inclined his head. 'The world is unpredictable, Meryall. From what you have said of the dead man, he was not without enemies. There are many details we do not know at present.'

The stranger began to stir and Hew came into the kitchen, having been out already to tend to the horses and ensure they were fed and watered, ready for them to make an early start.

Meryall looked out of the window at the long road stretching away from the house. She hoped that their path would bring answers to their questions.

Their journey passed without difficulty and they reached Samlesbury by noon, Hew leading their horses into the Sunn Inn's stables whilst they went in through the main doors. Eda was stirring a large pot of stew as they entered. She looked up and recognised them, welcoming them with pleasure.

'Please, come in and be seated. I will bring you drinks. I see you are without Madoc this time,' she said to Meryall. 'Introduce me to your friends, although one of them is known to me already.'

Meryall turned round in surprise. Arledge's expression mirrored her own. 'Known to you already?' she queried.

'Oh yes, I never forget the faces of my guests. How are you, Henry? I was unsure if you were coming back.'

The stranger started in surprise at being addressed. 'Henry?' he said distantly. 'That is my name?'

Eda paused mid-step, with a flagon of mead in her hands. 'Of course it is your name! Your friend is here, he has been looking for you.'

The stranger sat down abruptly. His face had turned pale and sweat stood on his brow.

'Henry.' He repeated his name again and again like a mantra.

Meryall sat down next to him and put her arm around his shoulders. He trembled as if his very bones were chilled.

'Henry… Now we know your name. This is good news,' she said.

Meryall caught Arledge's eye. 'I wonder if you could ask Eda if Hew is finished with the horses,' she said, her tone conversational. Arledge went into the kitchen, his steps uncharacteristically hurried.

'Does the name mean anything to you? Does it carry any memories?' Meryall asked.

Henry shook his head. 'No, it is unnerving to be

greeted by a name that you are told is your own, but which is as foreign to you as that of any stranger you might chance upon in the street.'

'Here.' Meryall helped Henry to his feet. 'Come and sit closer to the fire, you are shaking.'

Henry took a seat by the fire, the warm light illuminating his face and showing the shadows of fatigue that had begun to smudge the boyish eyes.

The heavy inn door creaked. Meryall looked up, expecting to see Arledge and Hew. A handsome young man, whose rich brown curls and merry eyes were familiar to her, stood before her.

'Brother Florian!' she said. 'It is an unexpected honour to see you again. I had not thought to meet with you in these parts so soon. Your path was on to York, I recall, when I met you in Lune.'

The young man was studying Henry. He roused himself and returned Meryall's greeting civilly. 'You are correct, Mistress Meryall, however university business brought me and my friend here to Samlesbury. Henry, where have you been? I have been searching for you for some time.'

Henry sat looking at Florian with a dazed expression.

'Your friend has met with a misfortune,' Meryall said, watching Florian's face closely as she spoke. 'He took a blow to the head and was unable to remember his name or how he came to be wandering in the woods when I found him.'

Florian's face was a picture of studied surprise.

'Indeed! Then he is most lucky to have met you.' He looked towards the window. 'In this weather, he would have been in grave danger of freezing to death.'

Meryall inclined her head. 'Luckily our paths crossed just as the snow began to fall heavily. We were near to a hunter's hut and sheltered there until my friends came looking for me, knowing I was on the road to Poltun. We have since been tending to Henry's injuries and trying to help him recover his memory, as a matter of urgency.' She thought there was a flicker of panic in Florian's expression of wide-eyed, innocent interest when she mentioned that there was an urgent need to recover Henry's memories. 'The only thing that Henry could recall was that he had recently visited this place. We have been waiting for the roads to clear and for Henry to recover sufficiently to travel to come here seeking answers.'

'Of course, you must have been keen to find out who Henry was and where he came from, lest there were people searching for him,' Florian said.

'Indeed,' Meryall replied. She sensed Florian to be playful and intelligent, but there was a glimmer of something she could not quite trace in the depths of his eyes, which she had not observed when she had met him at Lord De Lune's castle. 'We will talk further on the matter, but now, I think, we are all in need of refreshment. Henry has unfortunately suffered from a feverish illness following his injury.'

This time, Florian's concern appeared genuine. He

immediately steered Henry to a seat and went to help Eda carry cups to their table. Arledge and Fujikawa took their seats, watching Florian.

Who was this young man really? When she had encountered him at the feast, he had appeared to be just a high-spirited, curious young man, bored with the constraints of his society and seeking to prolong his journey to university in order to have fun. Yet she could not think of how Florian could be connected to the stranger, Henry as he had called him, but there *was* something to be grateful for. They were now closer to finding the answers they sought.

Chapter 11

Henry remained pale and agitated as they sat eating and drinking. Eda joined them between customers, contributing what she knew of Henry. He had left goods at the inn. She brought out a little pack at Henry's request. It contained a quill, ink bottle, scraps of vellum and spare clothing. The clothing was sombre in colour and style, but of good quality. In the bottom of the pack was a book, which was written in a language unfamiliar to Meryall, the curling characters mixed with numbers. She took it from a puzzled Henry's hands and turned it over. Looking closely at the spine, she noted that several pages had been neatly cut from the back of the book. She glanced up. Florian was watching her closely. She did not comment on the missing pages, merely returning it to Henry with a smile, remarking that it was not a language she had ever seen written and that he must be quite the scholar. Henry returned her smile.

'Indeed, Henry is a fine scholar. We are both

engaged in studies at the University of York. Henry has an interest in mathematics and the sciences, but is also gifted in languages,' said Florian.

Henry looked at Florian for a long time, as if trying to trace his own history in the face of this man who seemed to know him so well.

'Well, it is too late in the day for us to visit the camp at Grimsargh. Eda, do you have rooms enough to accommodate us?' Arledge asked.

Eda nodded. 'Some of you will need to share, I have only a few rooms left tonight.'

'Henry and I will share, of course,' Florian said. 'That will free up an extra room, Eda.'

'No need, I will share with the stranger.' Hew had entered the room without them noticing. He appraised Florian, before glancing at Henry. Eda shrugged and went to ready the rooms.

'You have gained both a name and a friend since I saw you last,' he said. 'Things have progressed quickly.'

Florian gave a foppish bow. 'Brother Florian at your service.'

Hew nodded without troubling to introduce himself, accepting a bowl of stew and a cup of ale from Eda and seating himself at the table.

'I can remain here with Henry tomorrow when you go to Grimsargh. He still looks pale and should avoid unnecessary exertion, and spending time with me may help bring his memory back. I can tell him of our travels together,' Florian said.

'I would prefer that we keep our party together,' replied Hew. 'My sheriff has tasked me with guarding Henry whilst the murder is investigated.'

Florian's eyes shot to Hew. 'Murder?'

Meryall sensed tension between the men. Hew distrusted Florian.

'A dead man was discovered in the forest soon after we found Henry covered in blood that did not appear to be entirely his own. There has been suspicion he may have been involved in the man's death. Of course, the loss of his memory has complicated things further, hence the urgency of our journey here to retrace his footsteps,' she said, her face and voice carefully calm and neutral.

'Perhaps you know something of the man who died, Michael Blackmantle? He lived at the Christian camp at Grimsargh,' Arledge said, meeting Florian's eyes with his own for a long moment.

'I have heard of the camp, but cannot place the name,' Florian said, his brow furrowed with thoughtfulness. 'I would perhaps have recognised his face, there are many from the camp who frequent the villages hereabouts.' He turned to Hew. 'Perhaps it would be best you stay with Henry whilst the others visit Grimsargh, I would be happy to remain with you to help you tend to his needs.'

Hew took a long drink of ale. 'We will stay together as a party. I will neither leave Henry without guard, nor let the others go into a camp which may be hostile, given the recent murder of one of their number. You may do as you please.' He stood and returned his bowl to Eda, with a slight bow of thanks, but did not meet Florian's eye.

A delicate pink tinged the young man's cheeks and Meryall thought she could trace a hint of anger deep within him, but he merely inclined his head to Hew and replied, 'Of course, you have your orders, I quite understand. My concern is solely for the health of my friend.'

Hew withdrew after dinner, taking Henry with him to find their room and settle themselves for the evening. Florian excused himself shortly afterwards.

Meryall looked across the table at Arledge and Fujikawa. 'Did you catch sight of that book?'

'Yes,' Arledge replied. 'It was of no language I could understand.'

'I saw something similar in the Russian courts,' Fujikawa said in a low voice. 'I think Henry's book may be a cipher.'

'A code book?' Meryall frowned. 'Why would a scholar have need of such a thing?'

Fujikawa shrugged. 'I do not know, but I think we may need to watch Henry and our new acquaintance carefully. All may not be as it seems.'

They retired to their rooms. Meryall had a room to herself. It was clean and tidy, though sparse. She washed and undressed to her shift. She lay down on the bed, feeling with sudden force the tiredness of her muscles. It had been a long day and despite her physical exhaustion, her mind ran on, considering the new information that a few short hours had brought.

There was a knock at her door. Meryall sat up. 'Who is it?' she asked.

'Eda,' came the soft reply.

'Come in,' Meryall said.

Eda pushed the door open and came into the room carrying two mugs. She handed one to Meryall and took a seat on the trunk at the end of the bed. Meryall sniffed the cup. The rich scent of a deep, earthy claret filled her nose.

'This is a very good wine, Eda.'

Eda smiled into her cup. 'The inn is fortunate to be on the route of several traders of fine goods, it enables me to acquire small stores of luxuries such as this.'

'I am honoured to share such a wine with you,' Meryall said.

Eda sipped her wine. 'I wanted to speak to you without the others present.'

Meryall nodded. 'About Florian and Henry?'

'Yes. They had been here for some days when Henry did not return with Florian one afternoon. Florian made a show of unconcern, but I could tell that it worried him. There have been letters arriving for Florian over the last few days, signed with the seal of York. He has been out scouring the countryside during the day in search of Henry.'

'It sounds like he is a devoted friend,' Meryall remarked.

Eda hesitated. 'It would appear so. Yet there is something in Florian's manner that unsettles me, I cannot say what.'

'What did you make of Henry, before he lost his memory?'

'He was quieter than Florian. Earnest, polite and somewhat serious. They seemed an unlikely pairing, with Florian's gaiety and thirst for company and good cheer,' Eda replied. 'I cannot believe Henry could be guilty of murder. He appears so gentle and thoughtful.'

Meryall sighed. 'I have thought so too, yet Arledge reminds me that even good men may do evil when the circumstances push them to such a necessity.'

They chatted about Lune, the inn and the many interesting guests Eda had encountered, whilst they finished their wine.

Meryall sat for a long time in thought after Eda left.

Tomorrow, she hoped, would bring more clarity to the situation.

The ride to Grimsargh was not long. The group were mounted and on the path out into the woods soon after the sun had risen. Hew rode close to Henry's side, his eye frequently directed towards Florian, who rode ahead, chattering to Arledge.

Henry remained subdued, but looked around him with the intensity of a drowning man searching for a lifeline.

Eda had given them directions to the camp, but it was easy to find, even without them. Not far along the path, they started to encounter signs of activity. The marks of cartwheels scored the road into ruts and little clearings amongst the trees showed signs of cultivation. Many of their crops, Meryall thought, must have been ruined by the early snow. She hoped that they had other forms of income, otherwise the coming winter would be hard for the inhabitants of the camp.

They saw scattered groups of people in the distance ahead of them and the smoke of fires. A woven willow fence enclosed the cluster of roughly made buildings in the clearing, but the gate stood open.

Several children had run to the gate, probably on hearing their horses, and a knot of adults had joined them, regarding the group with suspicion and surprise.

Meryall scanned the group. There was an older man with a kind face near to the gate. She dismounted and led her horse towards it.

'We bring you news of one of your number,' she said to the man, bowing her head in respect. 'And we seek your help in establishing his fate.'

The older man, still vigorous with a thick brown beard and hair touched with grey but plentiful, eyed Meryall and her group.

'May I ask who you are?' he said, his tone brisk.

'I am Meryall Holt, cunning woman of Thornton Cleveleys. My companions will introduce themselves, if you will allow us to enter and talk more at leisure. We bring information I would rather discuss with you in private.'

The man gave a half bow. 'I am John Cumberwell, blacksmith and spokesman of the village. Come inside, you may tether your horses by the smithy.'

He gave a nod to the people around him, who pulled back from the gate to allow them to pass and went about their business, still giving nervous glances to the group.

John stood aside to let them in.

He bowed to Florian as he passed by. 'Brother, it is good to see you again.'

Florian immediately jumped down from his horse and engaged John in conversation, eagerly telling him news from Rome.

Meryall glanced at Arledge and Fujikawa. They were following Florian with their eyes. She caught Fujikawa's eye and he raised his eyebrows in an unspoken question. She gave a small shrug in reply.

Hew was also tracking Florian's movements closely, but he remained at Henry's side, helping him from his horse when they reached the smith's makeshift yard. They tethered the horses and found that a bucket of water and feed had already been placed ready for them by efficient hands.

Meryall sensed nervousness in the camp at their presence, but the people around her, for the most part, showed little hostility. Here and there, there was a flicker of dislike on the faces of the people of the camp, but Meryall owned that they had likely had mixed responses from the local villagers and may well have reason to mistrust those from outside their own haven, aside from their difference of belief.

John had arranged stools and chairs for them in the smithy. No one brought refreshments for them, which was unusual. There was clearly a limit to their welcome.

Henry sat at the back of the room in the shadows, glancing nervously around him from time to time.

'We come to bring you difficult news,' Meryall said. 'I am sorry to tell you that Michael Blackmantle was found dead near to Poltun.'

John met her eyes. She could trace no regret on his rugged features.

'How did he die?' John asked.

'He met a violent end. We come to seek more information about him to understand his death.'

John looked around the room. 'And why are you the people to bring us this news?'

Meryall compressed her lips for a moment in thought. 'That is a complex tale. I encountered an injured man when we were both caught in the blizzard on the road to Poltun and helped him to safety. That man now stands accused of Michael's death, but cannot remember how he came to be injured and alone or in the snow.'

John looked at Florian. 'And what brings you, brother?'

Florian smiled. 'These people are acquaintances of

mine, John. I seek to help them in their mission.'

John frowned. 'I am surprised to see you amongst cunning folk, given your vocation. I doubt that your fathers in Rome would approve of your activities.'

'My fathers bid me to learn what I could at one of the great institutions of this land. I am sure they would appreciate my diligence in ensuring that the people of the country have the opportunity to encounter a servant of God whilst I am here,' Florian said smoothly.

'Your god,' Meryall said with a smile. 'As we have discussed before, in more pleasant circumstances, we are not godless, though we do not share a belief in your god.'

'Apologies, mistress, I intended no offence,' Florian replied.

'And you, brother?' John asked.

Meryall frowned, glancing around to see who John was directing his remarks to. He was looking at Henry.

Florian stepped in front of Henry. 'Should we not speak to this Michael's family, John? They must have been concerned at his absence. We should not delay in giving them the news of his death.'

John sighed. 'If truth be known, Michael Blackmantle was not popular here. His rhetoric was filled with anger and punishment. Most here know a different God. That put Michael at odds with the majority of our people. There are one or two in the camp who had sympathy with him, but we tolerated him because he was a Christian and had nowhere else to go. Still, I should make an announcement to the community.'

John stood, indicating that they should accompany him outside.

'Perhaps the people of the camp can let us know what they can recall of Michael's last movements,' Meryall said.

The others filed out. Meryall lingered.

'Do you recognise the other young man who accompanies us?' she said to John, when they were alone in the smithy.

'Yes, he visited us often with Brother Florian,' John replied, holding the door open for her.

The people of the camp had gathered around the smithy. There were a few children, none more than about eight years old, and about two dozen adults. Meryall saw a little girl with long braids peeping from behind a line of barrels by the smithy. She smiled and waved at her. The child dropped behind the barrels again without returning her smile, but Meryall could see her looking out from a gap.

John stood in the centre of the group. He had a calm presence that commanded attention and respect and the group quickly fell silent.

'I bring you ill tidings. One of our own, Michael Blackmantle, has been found dead. The circumstances of his death are unclear, but it appears that his demise was caused by another. These people have come to find out who killed Michael. Who amongst us was the last to see him?'

There were glances of concern between those assembled, but Meryall could detect little shock or regret on their faces. John's assessment of Michael's place in his community had been accurate.

A young woman stepped forward. 'I saw him go into the woods early on the last day he was here. I was behind him for a little way, as I was walking into the village, but he took a turning off the main path onto one that goes deeper into the woods around a mile from the gates. I do not know where he was going. He did not speak to me.'

John nodded. 'Does anyone have any further information that could be of use in understanding Michael's last steps?'

There was silence. The mood of the camp was sombre. John raised his hand, giving permission for the people to disperse. 'We hold Michael in our prayers tonight,' he said as they turned to go about their business.

'Thank you for your time,' Meryall said.

Arledge and Fujikawa came forward and added their thanks, shaking John's hand.

'We should return to the road. We have a long journey ahead of us,' she said.

John nodded to a young boy waiting at his elbow. 'We have assembled provisions for your journey. God be with you.'

Meryall took the bag, surprised at the gesture. 'Thank you, your kindness is appreciated.'

They mounted their horses. Henry looked tired and grey and leaned heavily into his makeshift backrest. John regarded him curiously.

'He has been unwell with a fever and is just recovering,' Meryall said.

Florian called a farewell to John and they turned towards the gate and back to the road.

There was much, Meryall thought, that she had yet to understand about who Henry was and how he had come to be involved with Florian. Once again, more information had only yielded more questions.

Chapter 12

Fujikawa and Arledge left the group as they reached Poltun, Arledge having business in the village.

Meryall rode on with Henry, Hew and Florian. Hew continued to show a clear mistrust of Florian, but held his tongue.

He hailed a child as they came through the village and sent him running, with a small coin in one hand and a message for the sheriff in the other.

Alys came to the door as they approached Arledge's house and waved. Her good-natured face comforted Meryall. It had been a long ride back and Henry was looking increasingly pale and drawn.

Alys fussed over Henry, seating him by the fire and putting a cup of nourishing broth into his hands. Hew cast a final, suspicious look at Florian and went back to his station in the shed, where Alys had set him up a brazier of coals for warmth and a basket of food.

Meryall went into Arledge's study and took out ink

and parchment, intending to write to Madoc. Arledge's quills were jumbled together in his desk drawer. She sorted them and picked out the quill with the neatest nib, trimming it with her pocket knife.

The study door opened. Florian stood on the threshold.

'Am I disturbing you?' he said.

'No, I had not begun my letter,' she replied.

Florian took a seat by the fire. Meryall rose from the desk to join him.

'I am pleased to have an opportunity to speak to you alone,' she continued.

Florian's face showed only a polite degree of surprise, but yet again Meryall thought she detected a flash of some unreadable emotion cross his features.

'I find myself beset with questions about you and your part in the situation Henry finds himself in. It seems suspicious that a pair of young scholars should be spending time within a Christian camp, so far from their university.'

Florian looked into the fire. 'The world is perhaps more complex than you are aware, mistress.'

Meryall drummed her fingers on the arm of her chair. 'Do not patronise me, Florian.'

He met her eyes and grinned. 'Apologies. I forgot who I was speaking to for a moment.'

Meryall shook her head. 'And do not attempt to charm me, either. You are both more and less than you seem. I distrust the appearance of your frivolity and the pretence of your scholarship. Who are you and what connects you with Henry and the death of Michael Blackmantle?'

Florian bit his lip. 'I did not mean to patronise you by implying that there were complexities beyond your knowledge. It is a fact that there are complexities beyond most in this land that present dangers to all who reside here.'

Meryall sat back in her chair. She upturned her hand, gesturing for him to continue.

'In Rome, the most senior dignitaries recognise, on the whole, that it is better for trade and diplomacy for Albion to be allowed to continue as it is. Yet we know that within Europe there is a movement to use the mission to bring our God to your shores as a cover for seizing control of mercantile trade routes and to suppress that which your universities teach that they feel threatens their beliefs.'

Meryall listened. 'And you come to establish how far the fanaticism might find allies on our shores?' she asked.

Florian steepled his fingers before him. 'My mission here – and Henry's too – is to infiltrate the camps, under the cover of my vocation and our role as scholars seeking knowledge of the beliefs of the Christians, whilst feeding information back to our superiors to enable them to understand the extent of the risk to the status quo that these camps may pose.'

'And what did you find?' Meryall asked, frowning.

'That most within the camps are peaceable, earnest folk, but that a small number of radicals seek to act as catalysts to disorder.'

'Like Michael Blackmantle?'

'Like Michael Blackmantle,' Florian acknowledged.

'Did you kill him?' Meryall's voice was harsh as she spat the question at him.

'I am here to find out what happened to Henry. We are united in that cause,' Florian replied.

Meryall snorted, frustrated at Florian's opaque answer.

'And who is the master who pays to call your tune?' she asked.

'That I cannot tell you. But I can tell you that Michael was more than a lone wolf. He too had a master whose name and rank are far above what I can tell you.'

Meryall sighed heavily. 'And Henry? I find it hard to believe he is involved in all of this intrigue.'

Florian was silent for a moment. 'I did not lie to you when I told you that Henry is a fine scholar. He has skills that make him valuable to our people. He believes … or rather believed, that what we do is for the greater good.' Florian rose. 'And so do I,' he said, turning to the study door, 'which is why I am telling you this. Please, stop digging into Henry's memories. It is best he does not remember his history for now. I would like more time with him to help him remember gently.'

Meryall did not answer. Florian stalked from the

room, the breeze from the swiftness of his passage stirring the flames of the fire and sending them guttering and swirling, their shadows flailing across the walls.

Meryall sat alone for a long time. From the kitchen came Alys's lively chatter as she plied Florian and Henry with food and drink.

The study door opened softly. Arledge came in and took his seat by the fire.

'You were deep in thought,' he said.

Meryall shrugged. 'I hardly know what to think.'

'There are developments?' Arledge asked.

Meryall paused for a moment, unsure whether to speak openly of her conversation with Florian. Although she felt ambivalent about the information he had communicated, she had a sense he had shared it with her because he trusted her. Still, this was Arledge's house and she should be transparent with him. She owed him that.

'Florian came to me and told me he and Henry were investigating the Christian camps at the behest of some shadowy master concerned with the security of Albion,' she said.

Arledge raised his eyebrows in surprise. 'Fujikawa has told me of many such intrigues in the countries he has visited. I did not expect that our stranger would be embroiled in such a network. As you have often pointed out, he has an appearance of goodness and honesty.'

Meryall rubbed her eyes. It felt like years since she had slept, despite the early hour.

'Florian said Henry believed what they were doing was for the greater good. He said his superiors in Rome are keen to maintain the equilibrium in Albion, but that elsewhere in Europe, there are those who seek to tilt the scales in their favour, using religion as an excuse to seize control of our assets. He seems to firmly believe in what he does and given he does, I do not doubt that Henry saw their work as honourable and necessary.'

'I have looked into Florian's eyes and find there a depth and complexity I do not fully understand,' Arledge said, stroking his chin. 'Did he say anything about their involvement in Michael Blackmantle's death?'

Meryall shook her head. 'No, he was evasive on that point, saying only that he too seeks to find out what happened to Henry.'

Meryall rose, stretching muscles stiffened from the long ride. She wished she had asked Madoc to leave her some salve.

'I believe Florian is earnestly seeking to find out what befell Henry. I am less sure he intends to share that information with us,' Arledge said, also rising to his feet.

'Indeed. Yet I am unsure what we can do. Do you think it would be prudent for us to discuss the matter with Dye?'

'Yes, I think that would be wise. Let us do so in the morning. But now, Alys is preparing dinner, it should be ready soon.'

Meryall nodded and they parted. She climbed the stairs to her room, keen to wash her face and hands in the hope that the grubbiness she felt would be removed by water and the clean, fresh scent of the soap she had made, which carried the memories of her home.

Alys had put a jug of hot water in her room, wrapped in a shawl to retain the heat. Meryall poured water into the basin and took out her soap. The fragrance of lavender and rosemary lifted her mood as she rubbed the soap between her hands. A lump rose in her throat, summoned by a sudden longing for home. She missed Madoc. She missed Horn Cottage. She missed her garden, the crow, her village. She missed her bed.

Meryall blinked hard to chase away the unshed tears. She was here, she reminded herself, to learn, and after that, she hoped that there would be travel, an opportunity to see more than the narrow confines of Thornton Cleveleys and Poltun. Being away from home was a privilege and a blessing. There would be time soon enough to be at home without interruption.

Meryall washed, combed her hair and braided it neatly over her left shoulder and put on a clean, plain dress. Feeling better, she went down to the kitchen.

Alys was setting down bowls of a rich stew, made with mutton and parsnips, quarters of warm bannock bread and cups of warm, spiced ale. The kitchen was cosy and filled with the delicious scents of the meal to come.

Meryall took a seat next to Hew. Henry was seated opposite her. Although still pale, he appeared less drawn and tired after Alys's ministrations and a nap before the fire.

Fujikawa had joined them and sat deep in conversation with Arledge, his hand resting lightly on Arledge's. The clear affection between them warmed Meryall. She liked the apothecary and was happy to see their relationship flourishing.

She looked around. Florian was not there. Meryall stirred in her seat. She was not sure why, but it made her uneasy that he was not with them.

The kitchen door clicked. Florian came in, stamping cold feet and carrying the scent of the fresh air on his cloak.

'Sorry I am late, Alys,' he said, dropping a kiss on her cheek.

Alys ushered him to a seat at the table, bringing him a bowl and spoon, her cheeks flushed.

'Have you been into the village?' Meryall asked.

'Yes, I was keen to explore Poltun and see the inn and Fujikawa's shop,' he replied, taking up his spoon and eating with gusto.

'And to go to the sheriff's keep,' Hew added, his voice flat.

'Oh, and of course I paid my respects to your sheriff,'

Florian agreed, unruffled by Hew's interjection.

Meryall looked at Arledge. He was watching Florian and Hew with interest.

Henry dropped his spoon in his bowl. The sound made Meryall jump and drew attention away from Hew and Florian. Henry had put his head into his hands. Fujikawa went to him and put his hand on his forehead.

'What ails you?' he asked.

Henry shook his head. 'It is nothing. Just a sudden sharp pain behind my eyes. It is fading now.'

Fujikawa looked at his eyes and felt his pulse. He frowned. 'Tell me if you have any more of these pains.'

They returned to their food, the mood subdued. Alys cleared the table and put out a plate of parkin. Meryall was fond of the sweet, gingery oatcake and gratefully took the generous slice handed to her, glad of a distraction from the tensions in the room.

Tomorrow, she thought, despite Florian's warning, she must take a journey once more into Henry's memories. Now more than ever, Henry needed to know what had happened to him. How she would do this without Florian knowing, she was unsure. As far as she could tell, Henry had not told Florian of her attempt to use the cunning arts to access Henry's memories. Florian knew only that they had talked to Henry and had taken him to the place he could last remember. However, Florian was not someone to be underestimated. His handsome, charming face concealed a ruthless, sharp mind, she felt. Meryall remembered encountering him at Lord de Lune's feast. He had shown an interest and awareness in the cunning folk then and may be more knowledgeable than she might expect an outsider to be.

She would speak to Arledge. He might have an idea of how they may help Henry without Florian's awareness.

Chapter 13

The morning came sweet and bright. The last of the snow had melted under a cheerful sun and the usual dry leaf and ripe fruit smells of autumn had reasserted themselves, having cast off the mantle of an early winter.

The birds clustered the trees and sang a song of almost frantic gaiety, like the people of a besieged town after their opposition has been vanquished.

Meryall looked out. Turi could start putting the garden back in good order, she thought, after the ravages of the snow.

Meryall set out for the village, her letter to Madoc in her pocket. The fine day lifted her spirits as she walked, looking around at the green of reawakening life.

She dropped off the letter. As she walked past the sheriff's keep, a small boy came running out. He was about to pass her, but he appeared to recognise her and came over to her.

'Mistress Meryall.' He gave a little bow.

Meryall smiled at how seriously he executed the bow. She gave a curtsy in reply. 'I am Mistress Meryall. How may I help you?'

'Are you going to Master Arledge's house now?' the boy asked.

'Yes, my business in the village is complete and I am heading back.'

The boy beamed. 'In that case, may I entrust you with this message for one of your guests?' He handed her a sealed letter. Meryall looked at it curiously. It was addressed to Florian.

'Yes, of course, thank you.'

The boy grinned and turned on his heels, no doubt planning to spend the coin he had earned for delivering the letter on a scoop of roasted chestnuts from the inn or some toy from the pedlar's pack.

Meryall fingered the message thoughtfully. It was too well sealed for her to open it and a quick inspection under the bright sunlight did not show anything readable either. Still, it would be interesting to see Florian's response when she handed it to him.

Meryall hurried back, longing to find him.

The kitchen was lively when she returned. Alys had put out breakfast and their little party was assembled at the table. Meryall sat next to Florian. She took the letter from her belt pouch and put it on the table between them.

'A message from the sheriff,' she said.

Florian looked at her in surprise. 'And Sheriff Brereton makes you her messenger?' he said with a cold smile.

Meryall laughed. 'No, the boy she entrusted the message to saw me on my way back and thought to save his legs and keep the coin he had earned for delivering the message.'

Meryall thought she saw a flash of relief cross Florian's face. Was he pleased that her relationship with Dye was not more established?

Florian put the letter into his pouch, unopened. Meryall was disappointed. She had hoped he would open it immediately.

After their meal, Florian went to check on his horse. Meryall watched curiously from an upper window. A few minutes later, he appeared at the gate and made his way towards the village. Now, she thought, was her chance to try once more to help Henry unlock his memories.

Meryall asked Henry to join her in the study. He immediately rose and went with her. Arledge caught Meryall's eye and nodded. He would let her know if Florian returned.

Meryall pulled the door shut behind them. The study was filled with shafts of sunlight, which caught motes of dust and made them shimmer in the air.

'Are we going to try to regain my memories again?' Henry said.

Meryall grinned. 'If you are willing.'

'More than,' Henry replied. 'I know not what to make of my friend Florian, but I begin to wonder what I have got myself involved in and whether Florian wishes me to remember or not.'

'Then let us do what we can now,' Meryall said.

She seated Henry in Arledge's chair before the fire, draping her shawl around him to keep him warm.

'We have little time for subtleties today. Relax, breathe deeply of the smoke from the herbs I will put in the fire and we will begin.'

Meryall chose herbs from the jars on Arledge's shelves. Wormwood, to aid their journey beyond their physical selves, and valerian root to help Henry fall into a slumber quickly. She cast them into the fire, whispering a petition to the goddess for her help on their journey.

Taking a skein of red thread from the desk, Meryall sat at Henry's feet. She tied a length of thread around her own wrist and then around his, taking his hand and holding it.

'Breathe deeply, relax and allow yourself to drift into sleep,' she said.

Henry took a deep breath and closed his eyes.

Meryall felt him relax and the pattern of his breathing ease as he fell into a sound sleep. She allowed herself to grow and move beyond her physical body, reaching out to his aura with her own. He was stronger this time, his light clearer and more prominent. It felt like pushing through warm water as she stepped into his dream plane again.

Once more, she stood in the forest clearing, looking at the stranger. He was waiting, peering down a path as if expecting someone to arrive.

Michael Blackmantle appeared, walking down the path, anger on his cold features. Henry looked uncertain, but started towards him with his palms spread, as if he would placate him. Meryall glanced around the clearing. A movement in the trees near the edge of the path caught her eye. A child! Meryall started in surprise. A small, pale face peeped through the undergrowth. She traced the snaking movement of a long braid as the child moved. It was the little girl she had seen in the camp. The child was looking not at Michael and Henry, but at the path at the far side of the clearing.

Meryall turned to follow the line of her gaze, but there was a sudden shout from Henry behind her and the mist was once more pulled in tight around them as Henry's subconscious mind shut down in fear of the setting. Meryall fell backwards, down through nothing, landing with a jerk in her own body.

Meryall blinked, feeling the shock of being suddenly and firmly thrust back into her own physical self. She squeezed Henry's hand. He continued to sleep.

Arledge appeared at the study door. Meryall slumped in relief, tired and glad to see her mentor there ready to make things right.

He came into the room and sat on the floor next to her. He untied the thread around her wrist, taking Henry's hand in his own to untie him too.

Arledge frowned as he held Henry's hand. He moved his fingers to his wrist to feel his pulse and then lifted one of Henry's eyelids to look into his eye. Meryall watched him, dazed and drained. Arledge got to his feet and left the room for a moment. Meryall thought she heard him calling to Alys. Meryall looked up at Henry. She gave him a little shake, feeling the feebleness of her limbs as she did so. He slept on.

Arledge came back into the room, carrying a tray, which he set down on his desk. He took up a pot and poured a tisane into two cups on the tray. He knelt before her, putting the cup into her hands. Meryall savoured the warmth of the rough clay cup on her palms, helping her to feel connected to her surroundings and her body once more. She sniffed the tisane. She could trace motherwort, lavender flowers and perhaps violet leaf. Meryall sipped gratefully, the reassurance and strength that the herbs brought beginning to flow into her.

When she had drained her cup, Arledge took it from her and helped her to her feet, guiding her to the chair opposite Henry.

The door opened and Meryall's heart gave a brief lurch as she remembered that Florian was expected back at any minute. Fujikawa came into the study.

Arledge went to him and hugged him, whispering

quietly into his ear as he did so. Meryall strained to hear their conversation, but was too tired to ask what they spoke of.

Fujikawa appeared grave. He went to Henry and took his pulse and looked at his eyes. He shook Henry by the shoulder and spoke his name. Henry did not stir. Fujikawa set down his leather bag and after rooting around amongst the clinking bottles of tincture and dried herbs and roots, took out a long pin. He pricked Henry's finger with the pin, producing a tiny drop of blood. Henry remained passive and unmoving under his touch.

Meryall frowned. Something was wrong. This was no ordinary sleep.

'Why does he not wake?' she asked.

Arledge and Fujikawa looked at each other. Arledge shrugged and turned to Meryall.

'This is one of the risks we spoke of,' he said. 'Henry's memory must have been so powerfully distressing that his mind has closed down around the memory to protect Henry from the knowledge of it.' Arledge sighed heavily. 'He sleeps to keep his mind from knowing what his soul understands. It is an unnatural sleep – and difficult to treat.'

Meryall clasped her hands hard in her lap, gazing down at her fingers. 'This is my fault.'

Arledge shook his head. 'Henry knew the risk and was willing to take it. He will recover, there are remedies we can apply that the cunning folk have long used to bring a mind and body back into unity.'

Meryall sighed heavily. Her consciousness of the gravity of the situation stole over her as the herbs helped to clear her mind.

'What shall we tell Florian?' she asked.

'What indeed?' Florian had opened the door softly and stood at the threshold, glaring at Meryall.

Chapter 14

Meryall held Florian's gaze. The young man's soft brown eyes, fringed with their long, luxuriant lashes were blazing. She almost wanted to laugh at the contrast of the sweetness of his features and the intense anger rolling off him in waves.

Fujikawa broke the silence. 'Henry has done much over the last few days, he has overtaxed his strength and suffered a relapse. He has fallen into a state of senselessness. I suggest we carry him to his bed in the kitchen and make him comfortable whilst I prepare medicines for him.'

Florian's eyes narrowed. He opened his mouth to speak. Fujikawa interrupted him with a gesture of impatience. 'Will you help me carry your friend?'

Florian closed his eyes for a moment. He had regained mastery of himself.

'Of course,' he said, helping Fujikawa to support Henry. Between them, they lifted him. Arledge opened the doors for them, then returned to the study.

'What happened?' Arledge asked in an undertone.

'Before Henry pushed me away, I saw that there was a witness who may have seen Michael's death,' Meryall whispered.

'Florian?' Arledge said.

'No.' Meryall shook her head. 'One of the children we saw at the camp was hiding at the edge of the clearing where Michael died. I saw Michael advancing into the clearing where Henry was waiting, but it seemed to me that the child was looking neither towards Henry nor towards Michael.'

Arledge frowned 'Someone else was there?'

Meryall shrugged. 'I can't be sure, but that was my impression.'

'We should go back to the camp,' Arledge said.

'I was hoping you would say that,' Meryall replied with a hint of a smile. 'But first, I need to smooth things over with Florian and speak to Hew.'

Arledge nodded. 'It is too late to set out today, let us arrange things tonight and set off at first light.'

Meryall agreed. She paused. 'Will he be OK?' she said, her voice catching in her throat a little.

Arledge put his hands gently on her shoulders. 'He will be fine. At present, he is hiding from himself. He needs time to find his way home. We will help him with that, but first, we must act on the information you both risked much to get.'

Florian had taken a seat close to Henry in the kitchen. Fujikawa was preparing herbs at the table and for a moment after Meryall came into the kitchen, Florian did not observe her presence. She watched him looking at Henry and felt a surge of pity. Although she did not understand Florian and was suspicious of him, she could perceive his concern for Henry.

He looked up. Meryall pulled a chair over and sat next to him.

'I am sorry that I did not tell you we were trying to help Henry regain his memories. It was his wish, but there is something there that is too terrible for him to face right now. He sleeps to escape it. To help him find his way, we must try to find out the truth so we may know what it is he is seeking to turn away from.'

Florian did not meet her eye. 'I asked you not to do this.'

Meryall sighed. 'I know, but you are not the only party concerned.'

Florian rolled his eyes. 'You have no idea who and what is concerned. I see you are unable to leave alone that which you would be wiser to let go. Now, we must take the consequences of that.'

Meryall's face flushed and her eyes gained a dangerous sparkle.

'I feel it is you that has involved Henry in something he would have been better well away from, now he is paying the consequences for your actions,' she said, her voice tight.

Florian breathed in sharply, but caught his instinctive reply and instead let out a long sigh.

'Arguing does us no good. What do you suggest that we do now?'

Meryall thought hard about what to say to Florian. She was unsure how far she could trust him and did not wish to provide him with information that would allow him to sabotage their investigation.

'When Henry and I were trying to regain his memories, I caught a glimpse of what happened.'

'Indeed?' Florian said, looking down at Henry and straightening a fold of his blankets.

'I saw what I think was a witness to the murder, someone from the Christian camp,' Meryall said, keeping her voice neutral and soft.

'A witness?' Florian replied. His voice too was well controlled. 'How useful. We should speak to them, who was it?'

'I cannot tell, but would know them again if I saw them.'

'What did they look like?' Florian pressed.

Meryall turned away. 'I think Fujikawa's medicines must be nearly ready,' she said, looking over towards him. 'I propose that we inform Dye of this news and ask her to provide us with one of her people to ride with us to the camp at first light. Will you stay with Henry, Fujikawa?' Meryall asked.

'Of course,' he replied, rising and bringing over warm herbal compresses which he applied to Henry's forehead, chest and feet.

The deep, green scent of the herbs rose between Meryall and Florian.

'A fine plan. I will go to the sheriff now and ask her to provide a guard for our journey.' Florian rose from the table. 'No more … games whilst I am gone, please,' he said.

Meryall shook her head in annoyance, but held her tongue.

Arledge came in from the study carrying a stack of books and scrolls in his arms. He set them down on the table. 'I have several ideas of how we can help Henry, but I would like more time to study. I recollect reading of similar symptoms, in particular in those who have suffered a serious trauma.'

Meryall took a seat next to him and pulled a book from the stack. 'Let us spend this evening searching for more information, then,' she said. 'And at first light, we ride to the camp.'

Alys cleared her throat behind them. 'If you would be so kind as to take your books into the study, I will bring you some refreshments there,' she said, holding the kitchen door open.

Arledge laughed. 'Apologies, Alys, I quite forgot whose kitchen I was in.'

Meryall took up an armload of books and went into the study. Arledge lingered behind, speaking to Fujikawa before joining her.

'What, exactly, am I looking for?' Meryall said, as

Arledge set down his share of the books.

'I recall reading of people falling into this state – described as catatonia or insensibility – following the burning of a group of people in the village during a siege. Afterwards, the memories of what happened seemed so horrific that some dozen people fell into a state of unwakeable sleep. The cunning folk of several counties gathered, at the request of the village cunning woman, to share knowledge and to try to treat them. The record of the correspondence and the diaries of the cunning woman are somewhere in my books, but I cannot recall where I read of it.'

Meryall nodded. 'I think I remember my mother talking of a historic congress of cunning folk come together to heal the people of a great castle who had fallen to a mysterious sickness. Is that the same thing you are speaking of?'

'Yes!' Arledge said, throwing up his hands. 'Of course! Scarborough Castle.'

He rooted through the books and scrolls on the table, taking up a large, plainly bound volume. 'It is recorded in the diaries of the cunning woman of that town, Marjorie Hunnam.'

Arledge turned over the pages, running his finger over the lines rapidly as he searched. 'Here! I have found it, let me read it.' Arledge sat down and began to read aloud.

It is five days since people began to fall asleep. Thirteen people are at present lying in the great hall of the castle, which we are using as a makeshift infirmary, sleeping a sleep we can by no means bring them out of. The apothecary has visited and declares that it is a malady of the soul, not the body, and that none of his cures will have an effect on these poor people. I have tried administering stimulant herbal compresses to their feet and giving them drops of ginger tea, infused with the last of my stock of grains of paradise, given to me by a trader returning from Africa some months ago, to promote heat in the body and bring their spirits and bodies back together. I have journeyed in search of their souls, but find that when I reach out towards them, they are shrouded in a thick fog, as if hidden from my gaze. None of my treatments have made any difference at all. The thirteen, six men, four women and three children, all remain in a deep, apparently dreamless slumber. We feed them drops of honey from a sponge and trickle warmed milk into their mouths to ensure that they do not die from lack of nourishment. I encourage my helpmate, one of the castle servants, to move their limbs often to keep their muscles from wasting away, but at present, I feel at a loss to do more and await the arrival of my fellow cunning folk, in the hopes that somewhere in the depths of our knowledge, we know a cure for these people.

Arledge glanced up. Meryall was leaning forward in her chair listening intently.

'The entry from the next day speaks of the arrival of the cunning folk,' he said, turning the page and starting to read again.

The cunning folk began to arrive at first light. Swithin, cunning man of Poltun, was first to arrive. Arledge stopped. 'He was the teacher of my teacher,' he said.

And after Swithin came Hilda of Samlesbury, Mildred of Scalby and Cenric of Cloughton. By dusk, as many cunning folk crowded the great hall as people lay sleeping. I am humbled by the generosity of the folk gathered here, who have travelled far and bring with them such knowledge and power I feel sure we can help our poor sleepers. Tonight, we met to eat together, to talk of what has been tried and to share knowledge of previous cases we have heard of where anything at all similar has been found. In the morning, we meet again to agree a plan of treatment.

Alys tapped at the door and without waiting for a response entered, bringing in a tray of steaming hot spiced ale.

Meryall took a cup gratefully and tucked her feet beneath her, waiting for Arledge to continue reading. He turned the page.

This morning, the cunning folk met. It was much remarked upon that such a meeting is a great rarity. Cunning folk are so bound to their villages that few travel. They often know the cunning folk of their neighbouring villages and correspond with their fellows, but it is rare for more than two cunning folk to meet. It is a shame, for meeting provided us not only with the opportunity to share our knowledge, but to pool our powers.

After much discussion, we agreed that we would

journey together, using the combined strength of our group, to bring the souls of our poor patients back to their bodies.

Swithin and Mildred brewed the herbs, whilst Cenric and I arranged a brazier of coals in the centre of the hall to light a great bunch of wormwood twigs, to assist us in walking beyond our bodies. The patients were moved into a large circle around the brazier and we linked them one to the other with a long garland of red ribbons, woven with hawthorn and rowanberries threaded onto strings. When all was prepared, we took our seats within the circle. Cenric led an invocation to the gods to help us in our task and my young servant friend and one of the cunning folk stood watch outside the circle, ready to come to our aid if we fell into difficulties.'

Arledge stopped, dropping the book to his lap for a moment, tapping his fingers against the page absently. 'They do not go into details about the difficulties they anticipated, however we know from our own knowledge what dangers there can be.'

Meryall nodded, remembering the unpleasant silence and barrenness of the place beyond places she had become trapped in on a previous journey.

Arledge smoothed the page before him and continued.

I can only tell what I saw with my own eyes with any accuracy. Though others have since told me their own version of events, the experience was so strange that it is difficult to form words around it. When we sat and joined our energies, the air felt slippery with our combined power.

I experienced a surge of confidence, a sense we were limitless. Yet when we focused our energies on the sleeping ones before us, there was still only mist. It was as if the smoke of the fire that had terrified them hung heavy on their souls. I walked towards where I thought my nearest sleeper would be. As I reached the edge of the mist, a hand reached out, pale and thin – a woman's hand. I put my hands out towards her, ready to pull her free, but as I advanced, she turned her hand palm out in a gesture of dismissal and I was thrust forcefully back. I tried once more, but again was pushed away from her. Turning, I found Cenric at my side. He too could not reach the sleepers beyond the mist. We looked at each other with frustration and puzzlement, until I recalled an old story my mother had told me, of cunning folk joining their strength within a journey. Cenric and I took hold of each other's hands and reached out as if we were going into a dream walk, a further layer of connections beyond the connection we had already forged. We emerged joined, a heady feeling of transience and insubstantiality I could easily have become lost in, had not Cenric been there as an anchor at my side. With our combined spirits, we reached out as one towards the sleepers. This time, our hands pushed easily through the smoke and we were able to pull out the first of the sleepers, a young woman. She wept and would have gone back into the fog if we had not held her from it and guided her back to her own body. This done, we separated once more, to rejoin the others and communicate to them how we had achieved the rescue of our sleeper. All were recovered. Now, we all rest, awoken sleepers and cunning folk, exhausted by our endeavours.

Arledge closed the book. Meryall met his eye. They both understood what they must do. It would be risky, particularly if they were unable to find a third cunning man or woman to watch over them as they journeyed.

Arledge stood, stretching. 'Well, before we try to help Henry, we must go to the camp. Tonight, I will send out messages to the cunning folk of the villages near here, requesting that they assist us in our work. With the will of the gods, when we return, we will find help awaiting us.'

Meryall rose too. 'Thank you, Arledge,' she said. 'I am humbled by your kindness.' Her heart beat hard in her chest. There was much to be done and she silently prayed that she had strength and skill enough to do it.

Chapter 15

The dawn light found Meryall dressed and waiting. She had slept little and her eyes were shadowed and her face was pale. She combed her hair and rebraided it, not because it had been untidy, but purely to give her something to occupy her mind. Her thoughts raced over the days to come. The journey to the camp would be difficult, her relationship with Florian was tense, but the task she must undertake with Arledge on their return was still more formidable.

Hew put his head around the door. He was to remain with Henry, but had helped Dye's stable boy prepare their horses and had them waiting in the yard. Dye had arranged for another of her guards to meet them at the crossroads as they made their way onto the road to the camp.

Meryall put on her cloak and a pair of gloves. Florian joined them and Arledge emerged from his study, taking his cloak from a peg in the hall and putting on a round fur-edged hat.

Hew bid them goodbye, with an air of resentment that he need let Florian out of his sight, but returned to the kitchen, where Meryall had observed with amusement that Alys appeared determined to feed him and Fujikawa and make much of them for the day, whilst they looked after Henry.

The weak morning light was obscured by a heavy mist that hung low amongst the treetops and over the fields. Meryall pulled her hood close about her face. She patted her mount, another strong, placid fell pony. His warmth and softness were comforting and she smiled as the pony investigated her fingers in search of a treat. She took an apple from her pocket and held it out to him.

Once they were all mounted, Florian led the way onto the road. He had spoken but a few words to Meryall since their argument about Henry, but this morning made a show of cheerful good humour and talked with animation to Arledge as they rode. Meryall rode behind them, watching Florian closely. She could not make him out. He seemed both good and dangerous, frivolous yet unknowable. The handsome, carefree young scholar she had met in Lune was something else entirely, but what?

She shook her head at her thoughts, trying to focus instead on the guard who was waiting for them at the crossroads. It was an older man, a scar-faced warrior she had seen before, usually close to Dye's side. He joined them, with a wordless nod, falling in to their party and taking up a position behind Meryall, who found herself suddenly missing Hew's familiar presence.

They increased their pace. The road was smooth and the conditions good. If they kept up a decent speed, they would make Grimsargh and be back in Poltun before the light failed them.

Meryall allowed herself to become lost in the movement of her horse, the scent of the air and the landscape around her giving her some peace from the heavy thoughts that had kept her eyes from closing the night before.

They paused briefly to water the horses and take refreshments at the banks of a stream, but were soon back on the road.

Meryall recognised the forest path to the camp as they approached it. The camp was evidently aware of their approach for the gates were pulled open as they neared.

John stood, sturdy and silent, awaiting their arrival. At his gesture a group of boys ran forward and helped them dismount and took the ponies to be watered and fed.

'Do you bring news about Michael's death?' he asked.

'We come to seek information,' Meryall said.

John frowned. 'None here have anything further to say, we have told you all we know.'

Meryall bowed her head for a moment. Her eye had caught the movement at the edge of the crowd. She held out her hand.

'Come, child, you are safe, you need to tell us what happened.'

The girl came forward nervously, her hands held tightly before her. John stepped in front of her.

'You may not speak to our children. They have nothing to do with this,' he said, his face flushed.

Meryall looked up at him. 'John, let the girl talk.'

John inflated his chest and stood solidly in front of the child, his face set in graven lines, eyes locked on Meryall. The child's hand snaked around John's side, the little fingers finding their way into his huge, rough grip. He broke his gaze and turned to look at the girl. She looked up at him and gave a watery smile.

John looked at Florian, who shrugged. John moved aside and pushed the girl gently towards Meryall.

'Tell me what happened,' Meryall said again, kneeling to speak to the child face to face. The girl's freckles stood out against the paleness of her face.

She looked up at John, who nodded encouragement.

'I saw Henry go into the woods. I liked him and followed him for a game, staying out of his sight. I was going to jump out and surprise him when he stopped. He went to a clearing and I hid, but before I could jump out, I heard someone else coming. Michael Blackmantle came up the path into the clearing. He shouted at Henry and knocked him to the ground and was about to come at him with a knife, but that man—' the girl turned to look at Florian '—came running and took Michael's knife off him and stabbed him with it.'

There was silence in the camp.

Meryall turned to Florian. 'Well, Florian? Is this true?'

Florian came to the child, whose eyes were brimming with tears, and gave her a pat on the head. He took a coin from his pocket and gave it to her. 'Never mind, sweetling, don't be sad, you aren't in trouble.'

He straightened up. 'Yes, it is. And now you must be satisfied with telling Henry that which will exonerate him, but which will also cause him pain. His mission that day was to assassinate Michael, but he lost heart and almost lost his life.'

The blood drained from Meryall's face. She felt Arledge's hand on her arm.

'What?' she whispered.

Florian sighed and shook his head. 'Come, let us go to John's hut so we may talk.'

They went into the hut. It was shadowy and cold. Meryall was shaking, but the cold was within the pit of her stomach, not the chill of the day. John saw her shivering and hastened to bring coals for the brazier.

She sat on the edge of a table, waiting for Florian to speak.

'There is much that you do not understand about the workings of Albion. Much happens to keep your world safe and peaceful that the people never know of. Mine and Henry's work falls into that category of clandestine endeavours to keep the peace.'

'Peace?' Meryall snorted. 'A man has died!'

Florian smiled. 'Many men must die for peace to reign.'

Arledge raised an eyebrow. 'Are we to take it you and Henry are agents of the council of chiefs?'

'I cannot tell you of my masters, but suffice to say my church in Rome is aligned with the purpose of the very highest orders in your land in this matter.'

'How did Henry become involved in all of this?' Meryall said.

'I did not lie when I spoke of Henry's skills as a linguist and mathematician. I was sent to York with the mission of identifying individuals there who had the skills needed to further the agenda of our shared masters. And Henry ... well, in a time where covert communication is needed, his skills are invaluable to us,' Florian replied, spreading his hands and smiling.

'And the skills you sought to teach him extended to murder?' Meryall snapped, her patience draining away.

Florian held her eye. There was a flintiness in his gaze, masked by the attractiveness of his face and the habitually sweet expression.

'Michael Blackmantle was an agitator. He was attempting to cause problems within the Christian community here, to raise sedition and encourage disobedience. He too had a master beyond the realm of Albion. As we discussed when we first met at Lune, there are parties who would seek to use Albion's unchristianised state as an excuse to seize control of its rich assets.'

'Why did you not seek to take him into custody? Or to kill him yourself? Why ask Henry to do it? I cannot believe he would want to do such a thing.'

Florian gave a harsh bark of laughter. 'Yet you readily believe I would? I am flattered, mistress.' He gave a half bow. 'Our masters provide orders. It is our duty to follow them. I have had the task of training Henry and this was to be part of his training. He understood the nature of our task and the greater good at stake.'

Meryall sighed, suddenly saddened. Florian, for all his bluster, was barely more than a boy himself; he couldn't be more than twenty-one or twenty-two years old. It was the shadowy figures above him she should feel angry with. And yet, evidently there was much that she did not understand about her world. She caught a glimpse of a door to another part of Albion, a part which she and much of the population lived in happy ignorance of, but which these men, Florian and Henry, had entered, ostensibly to maintain the equilibrium of her country.

'How did Henry come to be wandering alone?' Meryall asked.

Florian rubbed his face. He was pale and shadows showed under his eyes. Meryall noticed for the first time the signs of strain and worry on his features.

'I checked that Michael was dead, found that Henry was unconscious, having suffered a blow to the head. We were both covered in blood, for the wound in

Michael's chest had bled heavily and initially I feared that Henry too was dead. Satisfying myself that he was alive, I changed my clothes and went to the camp, where I told John what had happened – he had alerted my masters to Michael and acted as our contact here. I collected our horses and came back to the clearing. I put Henry before me on my horse and lashed Michael to the other, intending on finding a place to conceal Michael's body. Finding a place deep in the woods, I set Henry down under a tree and went to collect branches and twigs to cover the place I intended to bury Michael.'

Meryall noticed that Florian's matter-of-fact voice faltered a little and she wondered who had recruited him to his work. A clever, handsome young man with connections in the Church and the charm to ingratiate himself with people, Meryall imagined some shadowy political figure seeing a worthy puppet in Florian.

'When I returned to the clearing, Henry was gone! Our horses were still there, so I imagined that he must have woken, heard people nearby and thought he might have a better chance in the deep woods on foot if people pursued us. I could not tell where Henry had gone, so I quickly covered Michael over with the branches and mounted up, heading back to the camp, where I dispatched a message to our masters with a request for instructions. I then headed back to the Sunn Inn, where I expected Henry would meet me.'

'But then the snow started,' Meryall added.

'But then the snow started…' Florian agreed. 'I could not go back to bury Michael and became increasingly worried about Henry.'

Meryall looked at Arledge. It was clear why Henry would not awaken – he was hiding this knowledge from himself. Bringing him back to himself would be a bleak task. He would give them no thanks for it and Meryall wondered if he would be better off continuing not to know of it.

'And this was why you did not wish me to help him get his memories back? You sought to protect your secrets, or rather the secrets of the intrigues you have engaged in at the behest of your masters.'

Florian closed his eyes for a moment. 'Your interference has been unfortunate, mistress. But Henry would have perished without you, so for that I am grateful.'

'Yes, your masters would have been unhappy to have lost his valuable talents.'

Florian's eyes blazed. 'Whatever you may think of me, I care about Henry and would seek to protect him.'

Meryall felt the anger radiating from Florian. She smiled. It was a clean, sincere emotion and she liked him the better for it.

'Well, we must bring him back to consciousness, so whether it is for the best or not, it is time that Henry was reconciled with his memories of that day.'

'I will await news at the sheriff's keep. Have word sent immediately when Henry is awakened,' Florian said. 'I would not impose upon whatever arcane ceremonies you must indulge in to revive him,' he added, his mouth twisted into a hard smile. 'I have my limitations.'

He flung his cloak about his shoulders and strode from the room.

Chapter 16

The journey back to Poltun dragged. Meryall concluded that Dye knew of Florian's status, for the guard seemed unfazed by his revelations and rather appeared to look to Florian for instruction.

Arledge was quiet, the lines of his face drawn into a heavy frown. Meryall could not keep her thoughts from the terrible duty before her. Henry, she concluded, was a good man. He must have believed he was doing his duty and that his mission was important. She shook her head. She could not say it was not, though she could not countenance murder as the solution to any matter. Meryall felt as if she had approached the banks of what she had thought to be a gentle stream and looking down had instead seen a raging torrent. The world was not as she had thought it to be. How could she understand what was necessary and right and what was not? What might the consequences of Michael Blackmantle succeeding in raising dissent have been for the camp and even more widely for the well-being of

Albion? Florian had hinted at the political black clouds that were gathered on the edge of their horizon. Who could tell what lives might have been lost if he had not removed Michael from the equation?

Meryall wished she could close her eyes against the glimpse of the world she had caught, but she could not unsee it.

They reached the path to Poltun as the last light of day was fading away. Dye's guard left them and returned to report to the keep.

Arledge's house was lit cheerfully and smoke curled from the chimneys. Alys had hung a lantern from the hook in the old porch, which threw out panels of light, swaying slightly in the breeze.

Arledge pushed the door open and was greeted by Alys, taking his cloak and hat and giving him news of the village and details of the many refreshments she had prepared. Arledge kissed Alys's cheek and smiled at her, before moving on into the kitchen.

Florian and Meryall remained in the hall for an awkward moment, silence hanging in the air between them.

The study door opened. Meryall laughed with delight and rushed forward. Madoc stepped forward to meet her and took her in his arms. She felt his warmth as she pressed her face against his neck before tipping up her face to kiss him.

Florian had quietly walked past them into the kitchen. Madoc gave a wry half smile, clearly observing that Florian had not greeted him. Meryall shrugged and shook her head. Florian's disgruntlement with her was making him unusually rude.

Alys had seated Florian and Arledge at the kitchen table. Fujikawa stood at Arledge's side, his nimble fingers rebraiding Arledge's long white hair as he spoke.

'Henry continues much the same.'

Meryall took a seat, eager to hear Fujikawa's updates.

'But we have had visitors arrive whilst you were gone who I hope may help us.'

Meryall looked sharply at Arledge, who grinned at her expression and spread his hands.

'I did not want to say anything in case they could not come,' he said apologetically.

Alys was filling tankards with foaming lambswool, the spice and tangy scent of apples permeating the air.

'Shall I ask our guests to join us in the kitchen, or will you go through to the study?' she asked Arledge.

'Let us go through to the study, so we are not in your way,' Arledge replied.

He took Meryall's arm and squeezed it. 'Come, let us see who has answered my call for help.'

He opened the study door. There were two men and two women within who Meryall did not recognise. She regarded them closely. They were undoubtedly cunning folk; she could tell by the feel of them.

Arledge went to each of them and embraced them, thanking them for coming. He turned to Meryall. 'Well, it is not the great congress of Scarborough, but I think we have friends enough here to help us on our mission to help Henry.'

Meryall smiled, touched by Arledge's efforts. He must have sent word to every village around Poltun to ask for the help of the cunning folk.

They spent the evening in talk; it was too late to begin their work now and Alys's judicious efforts secured everyone present a blanket and a warm place to put their head for the night.

Meryall went up to the attic and undressed, combing out her hair slowly, looking out at the bright light of the moon. Madoc washed his face and hands and undressed, waiting for her in the narrow bed. She joined him, giggling as they struggled to find a position where they both fitted without a part of them falling off the bed. They settled for both lying on their sides, Meryall curled against Madoc's stomach, enjoying the warmth of his body against hers.

'Where shall our adventures take us?' Madoc whispered into her ear.

Meryall thought of all of the places that she had heard tales of.

'We must go to the markets of Constantinople, to see the fierce blue sky above the city, smell the spices and hear the wild, unfamiliar songs sung there,' she said, her mind's eye roving over her imagined city.

'Ah, yes!' Madoc agreed. 'We will travel east, Jura may be able to give us passage on one of his ships to take us on the first leg of our journey.'

Meryall liked Jura. Madoc's merchant friend had been a steady, reliable presence in their lives. Despite his rakish appearance and flamboyant lifestyle, he was dependable and kind.

'And if we spend such a long voyage with Jura, he may eventually persuade you to wear a gold hoop earring like his,' Meryall teased.

Madoc's chest shook against her back as he laughed. 'I begin to think that it is you who wants me to pierce my ear,' he said, nibbling Meryall's earlobe.

She stifled a laugh, worried about waking the others. 'Perhaps you are right.' In truth, she did rather like Jura's gold, pearl-laden adornments. Madoc's breathing grew softer and he burrowed his head into her shoulder sleepily. Meryall lay still, the events of the last few days running through her mind.

She was glad they had arrived home too late to start on their work today, for she dreaded the ritual they must go through. She feared that her own ambivalence to Henry knowing his history would cloud her ability to find him and bring him back. Her connection to him was the centrepiece of the ritual; she would lead with the others providing their power to urge her on.

Meryall's stomach knotted and her heart beat a fast rhythm in her chest. She took a deep breath in, steadying herself, and focused on bringing her thoughts to the present, to noticing how her body felt, feeling the tiredness and ache of her muscles after the long rides of the day, concentrating on Madoc's calm presence and the touch of his skin against hers. Her breathing grew peaceful and she drifted into sleep.

Alys woke Meryall soon after daybreak, bringing her a cup of fresh, warm milk. Meryall sat up with a start; she rarely had to be woken, the first fingers of dawn generally opened her eyes, but she had slept deeply, exhausted by the fatigues of recent days. Madoc had already risen and sat at the window, dressed, reading through the books he had carried with him from Thornton Cleveleys, seeking ideas for herbs to stabilise and calm Henry once he had returned. Meryall kissed him fondly. He caught her in his arms for a moment and pulled her into his lap, kissing her again. Meryall lingered, her head on his shoulder for a minute, until the consciousness of the task for the day intruded on her once again.

She washed and dressed quickly and arrived in the study to find the cunning folk seated around the blazing fire, chatting and laughing. They greeted her warmly. Arledge stood and gestured for Meryall to take his seat.

'We are gathered,' he said, turning to take in all of their faces as he spoke, 'to bring back a soul which wanders, in fear of returning to the truth of his life. Each one of you has offered your support in bringing him home. I thank you and remind you that this work is not without risks. Any of you who feel unable to continue, having heard all that is required, may leave without fear of condemnation.' Arledge paused. The cunning folk remained seated, eyes fixed on Arledge.

He turned to Meryall. 'You are to be the fulcrum in our circle – your connection to Henry gives you the best chance of reaching him. We stand at your side, lending you our strength in this matter.' Arledge broke off and beckoned to Madoc, who stood in the doorway. 'Madoc will monitor the well-being of the cunning folk. Fujikawa will be at Henry's side.' He took Meryall's hand in his own. 'I will remain outside the circle, so I am able to retrieve anyone who becomes lost.'

Meryall nodded. She was both relieved and dismayed. It comforted her that Arledge would be there to help if she needed him to – he had done so for her once before, when she had become trapped in the other place, but she would miss the feeling of his calm strength at her side. Her eyes prickled with tears, as a sudden memory of her mother came to her mind. She had been close to Arledge and had looked after Poltun for him when he had travelled, when she had been a young woman, and she remembered her mother's pleasure in Arledge's visits to them: the books they would pore over, the laughter and heated debates that flowed between them. Meryall's sense of the connections between the cunning folk here today, the generations of families who had known one another, had served their communities for hundreds of years, filled her with a sense of pride and awe. At the back of her consciousness, she felt the slightest tinge of discomfort, however. The weight of history also felt like a web of fine, strong threads, binding her in place, whether she willed it or no.

They gathered in the kitchen. A great pot of herbs was brewed – bitter wormwood, sour hawthorn berries and the green scent of vervain were tempered by a generous slug of honey. Meryall sipped her tisane. The familiar flavours soothed her, even as she felt the herbs begin to take effect.

They placed Henry, still slumbering, pale and with a faint, troubled frown on his face, on the kitchen table and arranged themselves in a circle around him. Arledge, Fujikawa and Madoc clustered at the back of the kitchen. Alys busied herself, straightening the house and folding blankets, anxious to help in any way she could, though she could not directly assist.

Madoc nodded at Meryall, his eyes warm and filled with affection.

Arledge had joined their hands with a web of red ribbons. Each cunning man or woman had a ribbon attached to their wrist, which connected to their neighbour, and another ribbon which connected them to Henry, the ribbons forming a crimson spoked cartwheel around and through them. Herbs were cast into the fire and the smoke drifted over them, lifting them into the other place.

Meryall shut her eyes and reached out of her body. She jerked back. The thrum of their assembled energies had hit her like a bolt of lightning, leaving her skin crackling with the power of it. She took a deep breath and reached back out, more cautiously this time, touching the edge of the other place where they waited for her. The force filled her, lifted her, propelled her forwards. They were all there, looking into the mist, waiting for her to reach in and pull Henry out.

Meryall walked towards the deep, swirling fog. It grew darker as she approached. The mist moved, pooled and ebbed like a vertical tide. She stared into it, tracing the shapes, searching for a sign that Henry was there. An unwelcome thought crossed her mind. What if he had moved into another place altogether, vacating his body forever, leaving it an empty shell? She had not prepared for that. Panic seeped into her spine, cold shivers contracting her stomach. The energies of the cunning folk moved closer to her, reaching out to calm her, to lend her still more of their strength.

She held out her hand, grazing the mist with it. Trails of it clung to her fingers and her hand left tracks through the fog, like riverbeds scoured into the earth by the flow of water. She closed her eyes, seeking Henry's essence. A thud, like a fist, hit her shoulder hard. Meryall gasped in pain and surprise, her eyes flew open and she saw a shape retreating into the mist.

'Go!' someone said, in a voice that shook her soul deeply, a voice of pain and despair.

'We cannot,' Meryall replied. 'It is time to come home, Henry.'

'Who is Henry? I do not have to go home if I do not wish to. I do not have to be Henry,' the voice came again, edged with anger and fear.

Meryall watched the movement of the fog and strode forward, plunging both arms into the dark mist, eyes closed as if she was reaching into fetid water. She grappled around, blindly, searching for something to catch hold of. There! She caught at a warm, moving thing and pulled, using all of her willpower and strength to drag the thing out of the mist, which pulled back like quicksand.

The cunning folk used their weight to pull Meryall back and a hand emerged from the mist. Meryall had grasped a wrist in the roiling fog and fought to hold onto it as Henry tumbled, struggling, out of the mist and collapsed at their feet, sobbing.

He looked up at her, anger and sadness distorting his face for a moment, before he vanished.

Chapter 17

Meryall blinked hard. Arledge had his hand on her arm and was staring down into her face with concern.

She glanced around. The cunning folk sat around her, untying the ribbons at their wrists, rubbing their heads, all of them pale and drawn.

Meryall jumped to her feet. Dizziness almost overwhelmed her and Arledge tightened his grip on her arm to prevent her from falling.

She stepped forward, with more caution, and put her hands on the kitchen table, searching Henry's face for signs of consciousness. Fujikawa was checking his eyes and pulse. He looked from her to Arledge with a worried expression.

Meryall dropped to her knees before the table, her eyes and throat aching with tears, tiredness overcoming her.

There was a rapid gasp, like a drowning man surfacing, from the table. Meryall stumbled to her feet, tripping on the skirt of her dress in her haste. Henry's eyes were wide open and he sucked in huge lungfuls of air. He pushed himself up and half jumped, half tumbled off the table, heading towards the back door. He threw the door open and they heard him heaving hard and sobbing.

Fujikawa pushed Meryall into her chair, signalling Madoc to come to her, and went outside to see to Henry.

Madoc brought a cup of water and held it gently to her lips, urging her to drink.

Alys had come back into the kitchen and was filling cups with a jug of spiced mead she had left warming on the hearth. Madoc took a cup for her and put the warm, rough clay cup into her hands, holding her hands for a moment until he was sure she could grasp the cup without shaking too much.

Meryall took a sip of mead. The warmth filled her chest and stomach, calming her and stilling the shivering of her insides.

She looked across the kitchen to the back door. She could hear Fujikawa murmuring soothingly to Henry, who continued to sob.

Madoc went to his bag and took out a bottle of valerian root tincture, pouring a measure into a cup and topping it up with warm mead. He went out and joined Henry and Fujikawa and after a time, Henry grew quieter and calmer.

Madoc led him gently back into the kitchen,

pushing him down into the camp bed by the fire. The cunning folk had begun to disperse soon after they had finished their drinks, the pressing concerns of their own villages and homes drawing them away.

Meryall and Arledge thanked each of them as they left, exchanging goodwill and promises to correspond and visit one another's villages.

Arledge pulled Meryall to one side. 'How are you?'

Meryall smiled. She sensed him checking her over, calming her energy with his own like a father smoothing his child's hair.

'I am tired. Tired and weary of this world, Arledge.' She shook her head.

'You have not seen enough of the world to be weary of it,' he said.

'My eyes have been opened and I cannot escape the sense of what is wrong in our country. I cannot find the old comfort and security I felt in the goodness of Albion, of our ways.'

Arledge stroked his beard. 'Sometimes, to understand our home, we must explore beyond our familiar horizons, see other ways of living and being.'

'Madoc and I have talked of travelling…' Meryall was unsure of how to continue.

'I have not forgotten that your mother's death prevented you from going with Madoc when he left on his travels,' Arledge said, his blue eyes soft in the dim light of the kitchen.

Meryall raised her shoulders. 'I had wondered if

Turi would consider staying on at Thornton Cleveleys in the spring,' she said, letting her shoulders fall and dropping her eyes to the floor.

She lifted her head tentatively. Arledge was grinning.

'I have been waiting for you to ask. Madoc gave me some very unsubtle hints about your wishes when he was here. I am quite sure that Turi will enjoy having freedom from this exacting old man for a little while longer.'

Meryall put her arms around him and hugged him hard. She heard a noise behind her. Henry was crying softly. Arledge caught her eye for a moment and followed her gaze to Henry.

Arledge spoke quietly to Madoc and Fujikawa and they, taking Alys with them, withdrew from the kitchen, leaving Meryall and Henry alone.

Henry lay with his face turned to the wall. Meryall took a chair and sat down next to him. 'Henry,' she said, speaking his name softly. He did not respond.

'I would talk to you, please.' Meryall tried again.

Henry sighed and rolled over to face her. He was pale and his eyes were still reddened by tears. 'What is there to say, Meryall? You did your duty and I thank you,' he said, his voice flat and hollow.

'Do you remember...?' Meryall said, her voice trailing off awkwardly.

Henry pushed his hands to his eyes. 'Yes, I remember! And now, though I remember, I do not know who I am.'

Meryall sat back in her chair, her heart heavy. 'And I have learned more of the world, yet now feel I know less than ever,' she said.

Henry turned to look at her face. 'You are tired. I am sorry for the trouble I have caused you, it is poor repayment for the kindness you showed me.'

Meryall shrugged. 'It is not your fault. What will you do now?'

Henry pushed his hands through his hair. 'Well, from what I can recall, I have a master and a duty which I should return to, yet I do not feel sure I can attach myself to that purpose as I once did.'

Meryall nodded. She remembered that fervent belief Florian had in the righteousness of his work. He was, though more rational, as zealous as Michael Blackmantle had been and would be as reckless about individual rights and happiness in pursuit of his goals.

There was a knock at the back door. Without waiting for an answer, Florian entered the kitchen, flanked by two of Dye's guards.

'Henry, you are well?' Florian said, advancing towards them, concern on his face.

Henry nodded.

'Good, then pack your things. Tonight, we start our journey back to York.'

Meryall stepped forward. 'He needs time to recover, Florian, he cannot travel.'

Florian gave a cold smile and pulled a scroll from his belt pouch, handing it to Meryall. It was sealed ornately with an oxblood red ribbon and wax. Meryall opened it and recognised a sigil of office. Florian had the authority of the highest council of chiefs.

She handed it back, anger flashing in her eyes.

Henry had been helped to his feet by the two guards, who piled his borrowed clothing and goods into the bag they had retrieved from the Sunn Inn and steered him to the door.

'He needs food and rest,' Meryall said tightly.

'He will get them soon. We are well provided for and will break our journey at the nearest outpost, where Henry can recover somewhat before we continue to York.'

'Why is it so urgent that he leaves now?' Meryall said. 'Surely a day or two here would not matter.'

Florian bowed. 'You are too kind, mistress, but you understand that now Henry has regained his memory, but remains in a weakened state, he poses a risk to us and must be amongst those to whom the communication of his knowledge is appropriate.'

Meryall shook her head angrily, bitter words biting at the back of her throat.

'I am sorry to leave you on these terms, Meryall. I respect your abilities and do not wish to affront you.'

Meryall could not meet Florian's eyes.

'I hope you can find it within you to consider the needs of the individuals who become pawns in your stratagem, Florian, for otherwise, you will find that your deeds grow ever more detached from the guidance of your heart.'

Florian bowed once more, then turned to the door, followed by the guards, supporting Henry between them.

Henry turned to look at her and call out his thanks and then he was gone.

Meryall sat down on the hearth and wept.

She wept for the world she had known, which seemed tainted by the powers which twisted just below the smooth veneer of the familiar reality she had been accustomed to, and for the two young men who had become part of that sinister world, for much as she felt angry with Florian, she called to mind that he too was merely a puppet to a greater master.

Tonight, Meryall decided, she would write to Madoc to tell her that Arledge approved of their plans. Her urge to travel almost overwhelmed her; the need for freshness and new sights filled her so intently that she was near running into the night, just to feel the joy and relief of movement.

She took a deep breath. Not yet. When the spring came, then would be the time to go.

Then she would find the world for herself.

About the Author

Prudence S Thomas is a psychologist from the West Midlands, UK and a lifelong book lover. This is the second novel in her fantasy mystery series. You can find out more about Prudence, keep up with her book releases and join her mailing list for sneak peeks, teasers and updates at her website: www.prudencesthomas.com